IN THE LAP OF ATLAS

In the Lap of Atlas

STORIES OF MOROCCO

RICHARD HUGHES

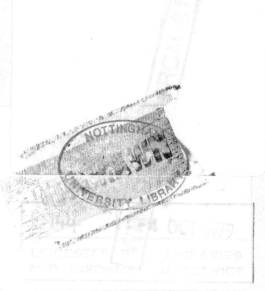

1979
CHATTO & WINDUS
LONDON

Published by
Chatto & Windus Ltd
40 William IV Street
London WC2N 4DF

*

Clarke, Irwin & Co. Ltd
Toronto

British Library Cataloguing in Publication Data

Hughes, Richard, b. 1900
In the lap of Atlas.
1. Morocco–Fiction
I. Title
823'.9'1FS   PR6015.U35
ISBN 0–7011–2430–X

Printed in Great Britain
by Fakenham Press Ltd
Fakenham, Norfolk

CONTENTS

Introduction

The Atlas mountains held an especial significance for Richard Hughes from early childhood. He always remembered his mother telling him the story of Heracles and the giant Atlas. His mind had been wandering a little when his ears caught suddenly the magic phrase: "He holds up Heaven on his shoulders!"

> That phrase struck straight to the core of my imagination. Before my inward eye, there flashed a vivid picture: the Cyclopean figure of the giant, his enormous hams based on half the desert plains of Africa—the clouds floating lightly round the straining muscles of his back—his mile-thick neck, bending like a willow under that unthinkable weight—the limitless blue vault which sprang from this single pillar. For I was given to seeing things like that, in pictures.
>
> The rest of the story passed unheeded. That huge, bastioned head, with its everlasting load, filled my eyes.

Both picture and phrase remained. And later, when Hughes learnt that Atlas was also the name of a North-African mountain-range, it was inevitable that those mountains should become invested with the magic of the giant.

It was not until the winter of 1926–7, when he was in his twenty-seventh year, that Hughes visited Morocco, and was able to compare the image he'd inherited from childhood to the visible reality. Then he found the splendour of the Atlas no betrayal of his child-imaginings, and a living source of mystery.

The writings collected in this book testify to the stimulative power of that mystery. Though few have been published before, all appear to belong to the period immediately following the publication of *A High Wind in*

Jamaica in 1929. For many years they lay apparently lost
and forgotten in an attic of the Hughes home in North
Wales. Then, in 1966, they came to light. Asked by their
finder, his secretary Mrs Lucy McEntee, if he wished to
include them amongst a batch of papers to be sold to an
American university, Hughes answered with an emphatic
No: they were to be set aside until he could find time to
prepare them for publication. But the opportunity never
arose: work on *The Human Predicament* precluded it. Had
he been able to set time aside to revise these tales it is
more than likely that some at least of them would have
reached the publisher in a different final form. This must
certainly have been the case with 'A Woman to Talk to',
work on which (Hughes told his daughter) was originally
abandoned when he reached a "dead end". Here, nevertheless, at last they are, constituting only the second
collection of stories by Hughes for adults. It is astonishing
to think that his first, *A Moment in Time*, appeared over
fifty years ago in 1926.

'In the Lap of Atlas' is certainly the longest, and
arguably the liveliest, of a number of articles written by
Hughes wholly or partly about his own experiences in
Morocco. Its status here as their sole representative is
consequent upon its author's habit, when aiming for
magazine publication in places as far flung as Great
Britain and the U.S.A., of deploying the same material
more than once. Thus 'Nightingales and Daggers in
Morocco' (*Radio Times*, 1930), 'Strange Christmases'
(*Harper's Bazaar*, 1930), 'Revolution in Tetuan' (*The
Graphic*, 1931) and 'The House in the Kasbah (*Vogue*,
1939), none of which are included here, all overlap to a
greater or lesser degree with 'In the Lap of Atlas' as well
as with one another. 'In the Lap' was drafted with
Harper's Magazine in mind, but for reasons lost in time it
never appeared in print. 'Strange Christmases', which
came out in *Harper's Bazaar*, highlights the same escapade,
but ranges over Hughesian Noëls other than Moroccan.

The Atlas "jaunt" in fact took place in the January of
1927—not over the Christmas of 1926 as Hughes states in
his account in *Harper's Bazaar* (a piece of poetic license
necessary there to his seasonal theme). After travelling
down the coast of Morocco from Rabat by way of Casablanca and Mazagan to Safi, Hughes and his painter
friend Jim Wyllie cut inland to Marrakesh. There, their
appetite for things Arabian was further whetted by lunch
with the Shereef of Tameslouht, a descendant of the
Prophet and a potentate whose enormous income was
guaranteed no less by his extensive plantations of olive-
trees than by the holiness of his ancestors. A visit to T'hami
el Glaoui, Pasha of Marrakesh, Hereditary Lord of the
Atlas, and later the most powerful Arab in Morocco,
followed swiftly. Hughes wrote in a letter to his mother
that his host was "as bad a hat as are made". Glaoui (to
whom this Introduction must return) was kind enough to
furnish the young men with a guide; but added that his
authority was not in itself sufficient to ensure their safety.
He was a man with many enemies. The next day they set
out. The experiences that followed possess an interest
beyond the intrinsic: for later, with some embellishment,
they became Augustine Penry-Herbert's in *The Wooden
Shepherdess*.

Hughes freely admitted that his return to Morocco late
in 1929 was his method of evading the *réclame* generated
by the enormous success of *A High Wind in Jamaica*. There
again, adventure lay in his way and he found it. He
reached elusive Taroudant, a destination denied him on
his previous visit. In the Valley of the Sous, at that time a
desert in the grip of drought and famine, he observed a
crowd of starving people collapse like a house of cards
when a push was administered to the foremost (the detail
crops up in *In Hazard*). He travelled south to Agadir and
Tiznit with a friend in the reassuring company of the
latter's father's professional assassin—a superior brand of
passport. And there in Agadir he quarrelled with the town

poisoner, who straightaway offered him tea. When Hughes protested at the crudity of his host's methods, the poisoner blushed but proceeded with the ceremony of pouring the tea, which he managed with the dexterity of a conjuror, his sleeves well rolled up. A macabre game began, one attempting to introduce the poison, the other to detect it. "In the end," said Hughes, "I managed, by skilful juggling, to acquire my host's cup. We raised our cups, made loud quaffing sounds, but drank no tea!"

The events that constitute the framework for the tale of Ish-ha in 'The Fool and the Fifteen Thieves' occurred during this stay of 1929–30. The description Hughes gives there of his camp in the cork woods of Northern Morocco is fuller than that which appears in the Autobiographical Introduction to his American *Omnibus* of 1931, but is substantiated by the latter. It must remain an open question, however, whether the alleged robbery actually occasioned Hamed's story of Ish-ha. A typescript, undoubtedly earlier than those of 'The Fool and the Fifteen Thieves' and entitled 'The Adventures of Sh-ha the Fool', groups together several anecdotes without attempting to link them in a consecutive narrative. Here we are told that Sh-ha was one of those fools and jesters "who beguiled from time to time the cares of the Sultans of Fez". In addition to the tales of the door, the fifteen thieves, and the bough, it contains 'The Laughing Ass':

Whenever the Sultan went riding, he used to take Sh-ha riding behind him on his donkey, for diversion. One day, before they started out, the Sultan sent a man to cut off the donkey's lips. When Sh-ha saw this, he cut off the tail of the Sultan's horse: and they started off without the Sultan noticing this.

After they had gone some little way the Sultan looked round and said: "What is your ass laughing at, Sh-ha?"

"He is laughing at your horse's backside," quoth Sh-ha.

'The Fool and the Fifteen Thieves' points in a general way
to the likely origins of Richard Hughes's Moroccan stories.
His camp, he says, "became a recognised stopping-place
for travellers," who often paid for a night's lodging in
music, or in stories "own blood-brother to those in the
Arabian Nights". A version of the 'Sidi Heyar' tale not
preferred for this book possesses a cork-forest camp framework, and is told to Hughes after dinner one night by a
one-night guest. Certainly it is difficult to believe (whatever the temptation to think otherwise) that the stories
printed here, with the exception of 'A Woman to Talk to',
are original products of Hughes's own imagination; rather
they strike one as being sensitive and consummate re-
tellings of tales that may well be alive still in Moorish oral
cultures. If this is so there is a nice irony in the fact that in
1944 the B.B.C. had 'The Red Lantern' translated into
Arabic for broadcasting from Teheran.

It is impossible, then, to pinpoint the precise sources of
these stories. The existence of two or more versions of
some of them, with and without frameworks and internal
narrators, and in one case, discussed below, of two versions
of a tale whose contrasting frameworks credit different
narrators with the story, leads one to the conclusion that
Hughes did not feel that a faithful representation of the
actual circumstances in which he first encountered a tale
necessarily served the best interests of his art. Nevertheless
it is likely that more than one was told to him by his
manservant Hamed. Mrs Frances Hughes, who spent
several months in Morocco with her husband shortly after
their marriage in January 1932, recalls the fact that
Hamed sometimes told them stories after bringing in the
last dish of the evening meal. Very villainous to look at,
very small, very dark, but highly intelligent, Hamed kept
up a fiction that he knew no English (which was untrue),
but talked French—in the future tense only! Hamed was
very dignified. He wore braided magenta trousers and a
braided jacket—the Hugheses bought him new ones every

year, which was no less than he expected from people of their station—and walked with a natural grace. He bargained in the market-place, lit cigarettes and cooked for his employers, but delegated menial household chores such as carrying home his purchases, cleaning the brass and sweeping up, to his ragged cousin who chewed opium. When Frances, convalescent with a mildly gangrenous toe, made it known that she was thinking about crutches, Hamed was shocked. Crutches were for beggars: she must have a stick with an ivory top—or a silver one. Hamed doubtless believed it his business to educate his Western employers into an awareness of his rich and ancient culture, and telling them stories was the form his instruction took. Which for the Hugheses proved an entirely painless procedure.

One of his stories concerned a man who was walking to Tetuan. Seeing a corpse by the side of the road, the man sat down beside it for two days and two nights; sat there without touching it or robbing it; and presently was arrested for its murder! The question of course arose as to why he lingered there so long. Well, said Hamed, walking for hours and hours, for days and nights, on a dusty sandy road, he'd seen absolutely nothing worth seeing. Until the corpse, which was hence of great interest to him. This anecdote caught the Hugheses' imaginations, for it demonstrated the gulf yawning between Moorish and Anglo-Saxon behaviour. But it was not one that Richard Hughes recorded.

It was during the visit of 1929–30 that he acquired his house in the citadel—the Kasbah—of Old Tangier. This was a Moslem quarter entirely: no Christian had owned property there since the time of Charles II, when the British had held the town.

The price of the house was two donkey-loads of silver. The man Hughes bought it from was so excited that he didn't go to bed for two days and two nights, but sat up biting every piece to make certain it was good.

But the arrival of a Christian proved extremely un-popular. "When I came to move in," wrote Hughes, "the neighbours complained that to have a Nazarene living in the street would send down the real-estate value of the whole district." The hereditary saint who lived next door, a magnificent and important personage whose Prophetic ancestry rendered him infallible, was thoroughly ashamed of his wall-to-wall proximity to an infidel. But eventually Hughes's neighbours became reconciled to his presence: for not only did he strictly observe the Moslem code of good manners—never staring at anyone, never glancing through an open street door, and above all refraining from mounting to his roof at sunset (the time when Moslem women go up to theirs to take the air)—but he showed himself ready to help them in their dealings with Authority.

The house required repairs, and after the customary and lengthy business of architects, plans and estimates, Hughes found himself a builder. In December 1931, during a later trip, he writes in a letter to Frances Bazley, soon to be Mrs Richard Hughes:

> I am now dusty, having been quarrelling with my builder, who calls himself Mulay (which means Prince) Omar, because he is descended from the Prophet, and carries bricks home in his pocket. I get dusty because if I didn't he wouldn't think I was enjoying the quarrel properly.

Here is the setting for 'Two Pots of Gold', the second of Hughes's stories to combine autobiography and fiction. It cannot be assumed, however, that Mulay Omar was in truth the source of the tale told by Mulay Ali in this book. In another version of the story entitled 'The Widow and the Djinn' the narrator is the widow herself, Fatima. Richard Hughes is sitting with his "Danish friend, Andersen, Chief of the little International Police Force of the Tangier Zone" when she arrives to pour out her woes. In this account the mason's name is Abdelkader. But probably the crucial difference concerns the story's *dénouement*. In 'The Widow and the Djinn' Hughes does not himself step into the tale to solve the mystery of the magician's disappearance; upon hearing of the powerlessness of the police where Djinns are concerned, the widow swears the mason to secrecy and insists "that he cover up the rifled hiding-place as if it had never been opened". She then does nothing to discourage certain rumours that get about, and in due course sells her property for an excellent price! 'Two Pots of Gold', with its greater length and extra twist, seems to be the latest version of this story.

With 'A Woman to Talk to' we depart from the vernacular Moorish story and come to what is undeniably an autonomous work of Richard Hughes's imagination. It is appropriate at this point to allude to matters of a purely editorial nature. Editorial work on the other thirteen tales consisted first, in choosing between different complete versions of a story in cases where more than one existed—choices that were not at all difficult to make; second, in tidying up the sometimes chaotic punctuation of the original typescripts; and third, in supplying a lacuna of two missing paragraphs (due probaby to a typist's error) in the text of 'The Country Parson'. It was 'A Woman to Talk to' that posed the most absorbing questions for an editor. Here, three distinct typescripts are in existence: I shall call them (a), (b) and (c). (a) is a wide-spaced typescript of 63 pages (numbered in two parts 1–6 and 1–57)—a complete version much revised and overwritten in ink. (b) is a typescript of 7 pages constituting a fair copy of some 14 pages of (a), corrected in pencil. (c) is a typescript again of 7 pages being in the main a fair copy of (b) but of slightly greater length in terms of the amount of narrative it contains and including towards its end a paragraph not present in (a) or (b); this script again corrected in pencil. The story as it is printed below is a composite of (c) and (a), the latter taking over where the former runs out. Editorial interference has been restricted to the making of what seemed to me to be the minimal number of cuts, adjustments and interpolations necessary to enable the story to run smoothly.

Certain questions, of course, are raised by the state of the texts. Since (b) breaks off in mid-sentence at the foot of its seventh page it is possible that a further portion of corrected fair copy has been lost. As things stand, however, it is (c) that raises the most interesting questions. Its extra paragraph (page 7) introduces a new character, an elder sister for the narrator. This fact opens up a whole dimension of possibility and implies that Hughes reached the "dead end" to which I have already referred whilst attempting a major revision of the tale. I have cut the extra paragraph for reasons that will be obvious when it is read; yet it is fascinating to speculate about the part this sister might have played in the story of a Prince whose harem of a thousand women contains not one to whom he can talk. For those who like to speculate, here is the passage: in (c) it follows the paragraph ending "the finest spearman of this our twentieth century" on page 100 below:

> My only regret was that my sister was to share this privilege. She was a narrow-minded and dare-devil girl, for whom I had then a contempt. Even if she did nothing, her very presence, I felt, was a disgrace to me, and would minimise me in the Kaid's eyes. It is true that there were those who thought her beautiful; but as her younger brother I thought, and often told her, that she had the face of a very ill monkey . . .

I have called 'A Woman to Talk to' an autonomous work of imagination; like all four of Richard Hughes's novels, however, it possesses strong points of contact with historical persons and events (a fact which does not, I trust, compromise its autonomousness). The narrator's uncle is based upon W. B. Harris, the correspondent of

The Times in Tangier from 1887 to his death in 1933. Hughes knew of Harris when he first went out to Morocco in 1926, and when he mentioned Harris's name found it to be as well known there as that of the Prince of Wales in England. Harris was nonchalant, witty and resourceful, and his life, containing more than a share of the bizarre and perilous, was one that could not fail to appeal to Hughes's imagination. After Harris's death his family asked Hughes to be his biographer, and he took on the task; yet though he conducted researches over a period of years, he never—for reasons now obscured by time—got further than drafting the opening of Chapter One. Amongst his research papers are a collection of 'Personal Recollections' of Walter Harris, some of which he probably had at first hand, since he came to know Harris personally during his periodic visits to Morocco. The anecdotes collected here conclusively demonstrate that the relationship between the narrator's uncle and Kaid Omar el Medouli in the tale is based upon the real-life friendship between Harris and T'hami el Glaoui. Here is a brief extract from the 'Personal Recollections':

Glaoui once stripped to show Harris his scars, and Harris said there was hardly enough of his body to put the palm of your hand on that was not scarred. (The curious droop of his mouth is due to the severing of a tendon in his face.) When Admiral Gaunt visited Glaoui and explained in his usual manner how he had won the war, Glaoui listened to him, apparently impressed. Then Gaunt caught sight of Glaoui's withered arm and asked him how he had come by it. Glaoui replied in a deprecating way that he had been toasting kub-bub over a charcoal fire when he was a boy and had foolishly slipped and burnt his hand on the stove. This was Glaoui's reply to the Englishman's boasting. For the truth of that withered hand, as Harris told me, was that Glaoui was once besieged in a fort which was about to fall to the enemy: he evacuated his men and remained behind alone to blow up the powder magazine as the enemy entered, and that was how his hand was rendered useless.

It should be added that a dash of the notorious bandit chief Moulay Ahmed er-Raisuli has been thrown for good measure into the conception of Medouli: for the episode of the Koran and the horses was acted out, with some differences of detail, between Harris and Raisuli.

'A Woman to Talk to' is not a seamless work of art: it never achieved its final form. Yet it contains memorable writing that could be by no one but Richard Hughes. It is characteristic; and the interest it evinces in racial differences is one that Hughes went on to explore in both *In Hazard* and *The Human Predicament*. I hope, therefore, that it will be felt to earn its place in this book.

Few of these writings have previously come before the public. 'The Fool and the Fifteen Thieves' appeared in *The Listener* in 1931 and again in the *Evening News* in 1950. A version of 'Two Pots of Gold'—much compressed and truncated—was used to close 'The House in the Kasbah'. 'The Red Lantern' has been anthologised and translated into at least one European language. In addition, 'The Widow and the Djinn', 'The Fool and the Fifteen Thieves' and 'The Nitwit' (a version of the 'Sidi Heyar' tale) were sold in 1950 to the B.B.C. for a single broadcast use over the old Light Programme. No evidence has as yet come to light to prove that any of the other stories have been exposed to an audience other than the Hughes family.

Finally I must acknowledge my debt, and extend again my grateful thanks, to those who have helped me in my researches towards this book: Mrs Frances Hughes, Mrs Penny Minney, Mrs Lucy McEntee, Mr Peter France—and my wife Sandra.

Richard Poole
December 1978

In the Lap of Atlas

I REMEMBER standing, one mid-winter evening in the year 1346, at the gates of a grim old castle. We had sent in a messenger to tell the Lord of the Land that two benighted travellers begged the privilege of a night's lodging; and we waited his answer anxiously, for he was reputed to be none too well disposed to strangers found in his domain. The hand of our man-at-arms fidgeted under his cloak for the hilt of his dagger: our three little page-boys, shivering in their ragged tunics among our mules, looked ready to bolt at any moment: and my companion and I lit cigarettes to occupy our minds. We had travelled far, sleeping in castle guest-room or peasant's stable as opportunity arose: but, thank Heaven, we had not yet run out of tobacco ... The huge iron-pleated door opened, and a gigantic seneschal appeared. He was black. He wore a long striped robe, had a silver earring as big as a bangle in one ear and a long curved silver-sheathed poignard at his waist, and carried a heavy bunch of keys in his hand. —Who were we, and had we letters of recommendation to his master?

Gentle Reader, this is sober, honest-to-God truth, and it is only a few weeks since it all happened—the year 1346 of the Mahommedan calendar being known to Christians as A.D. 1928. But we were in the heart of the Great Atlas, and it might just as well have been 1346 of the Christian era: there, things have not changed a tittle since then. We in Europe keep the Middle Ages (what is left of them) locked up in museums like animals in a menagerie: we take our children to see them, and feed them a history-book now and then, like giving buns to the bears: but in that vast and hardly penetrated range of mountains behind Morocco, whose furthest tall headlands are thrust

19

out into the great sand-ocean of the Sahara—in that
Upholder of the Skies, Atlas, prototype of all giants—Time
sleeps by his scythe, and the sands are suspended motion-
less in his glass. There, it is the modern traveller who is the
museum-piece. You might almost expect to find a pair of
stuffed tourists in plus-fours and tuxedos and elastic-sided
boots, with a polo-stick in one hand and opera-glasses in
the other, decorating some chieftain's hall.

We had *no* recommendation to his lord and master: as a
matter of fact, we were under the patronage of his master's
favourite enemy: so it was a case for bluff. My companion
produced an imposing-looking document from his pocket-
book, and handed it in with as haughty a frown as his face
could manage. It was addressed to him by name: at the
top was embossed a series of royal arms, with the words
'by appointment': and underneath was an urgent request
from a certain West End tailor for the immediate settle-
ment of a long-outstanding account.

A mean trick, perhaps: but there are times when one
can't afford to be too squeamish. If one had been thrown
out—well, one would not have landed soft.

The Black disappeared with the document. While he
was away, a small ragged child came out and humbly
kissed the hems of our garments. Then presently the
seneschal returned, and invited us in. No one had been
able to read English; so our bluff had not been called.

I remember that castle particularly for the cunning of
its defences. The narrow path approaching it from the
mouth of the valley wound round three sides, close under
the tall walls: and on the fourth side passed between the
castle itself and a curtain-wall on the edge of a river. This
wall protected the gates from a direct frontal attack, and
at the same time made it impossible for an enemy to give
covering fire to a party approaching by the path. But that
was not the only card they had in their sleeve. The
moment we stepped through the doorway we found our-
selves in darkness, confused by the sound of rushing water

somewhere at our very feet: we had to pause fully thirty
seconds till our eyes, dazzled by the daylight outside,
could see where we were. Suppose some enemy *had*
succeeded in rushing the gate by surprise: that half-
minute's dazzlement would give the defenders plenty of
opportunity of dealing with him: and the rushing stream
into which as likely as not he would stumble would carry
him out under the walls faster than ever he came in.

The big Black, however, guided us through this long
tunnel of darkness out into the courtyard, and from there
up a flight of steps to the upper storey of a tower in one
corner—the guest-room. It was spotlessly clean. Both
floor and walls were covered in a brilliant polished white
plaster. The ceiling was of painted wood: there were two
windows, whose lovely grilles of wrought-iron made a
wonderful pattern against the snow-capped mountains,
the crimson valley, the shining river winding between huge
ancient olive trees which the rapid African dusk was
already blackening.

The furniture of the room was simple: two mattresses,
some cushions, and a small but pleasing old Moorish
carpet. That is one of the charms of Oriental luxury—the
lack of it. Lay a rug on the floor, and put a few cushions
round the wall: your room is furnished. Kick your feet into your slippers at the door: you are equipped for a journey.
Unsling your dagger: you are undressed for the night.
Shake yourself thoroughly and straighten your turban:
you are dressed again in the morning. And finally, get
whacked hard enough on the head—and straight to
Heaven you go.

But Atlantean winter nights, many thousand feet above
the sea, are cold: and we had hardly sat down on our
mattresses when two more slaves arrived: one with a huge
candlestick of beaten brass, another with an earthenware
brazier of charcoal which he carried on his head. This he
set down on the floor in the middle, and soon blew to a
most comfortable glow. What your Arab really likes on a

cold evening is to get one of these braziers, put a few grains of incense on it, and then sit on the floor with the brazier tucked under his petticoats, sighing and grunting with delight while the grateful heat warms the very marrow of his bones, and the blue smoke of the incense comes out of his collar and curls about his ears. It is an alarming sight the first time you see it—as alarming as Sir Walter Raleigh and that first famous pipe of his.

But there is comfort coming for the inner man, too: supper is soon ready. Another slave brings in a big brass basin and a brass kettle; you stretch out your right hand over the former, and he pours warm water over it from the latter. Next comes the bread, in a basket or big covered bowl: the host or his steward breaks it, and apportions it round. Then the broad dish on a broader brass tray (perhaps a whole roast sheep, or a dozen chickens) is set down on the floor, and you all sit round it; and after each diner has cried out heartily by way of Grace, "*In the Name of God!*" you all dip your right hands very apostolically in the dish, the host extracting any particular tit-bit and laying it before the most honourable guest.

Now how many Christian cooks, I wonder, could roast a sheep (or even a chicken) so tenderly that you could pinch off a mouthful without difficulty between finger and thumb? Yet that is what these Moorish cooks do. I have eaten meat in Morocco at expensive European hotels which needed knife, fork, and then almost a shark's triple denture to dissever it; meat which made one realise how Morocco leather got its former reputation for durability: but without exception in the houses of natives I found it as tender as butter—cooked, too, with stuffings, with gravies tasting of spices and olives and cummin seed, that no *cordon bleu* would be ashamed of.

As each dish is finished with, a clap of the hands and it is carried away to the servants, and a fresh one set in its place, their order being so arranged that the more delicate flavours are succeeded, as appetite wanes, by the more

highly spiced ones: until last of all comes the famous
couscous. This is a tall cone of something white and mealy
(flour steamed over broth, I believe), in consistency like
milled chestnuts, generally sprinkled with powdered
cinnamon and sugar, and with roast quails or some other
such pleasant surprise hidden at the centre. There is a
great art in eating a couscous. Gather some of the meal in
the palm of your hand, shake it gently till it conglomerates
into a ball, then flick it neatly into your mouth with your
thumb. And if the ball does not refuse to form, or once
formed does not break and distribute itself down your
neck or in your neighbour's eye, you are much more
adroit than I am! After the couscous, back comes the
basin and kettle, and this time you wash your hands
thoroughly; and if you have a fine long white beard you
may now shampoo it, and comb it out all shiny and
fluffy and soft. At least, I once saw this done by the City
Fathers at a dinner-party given by the Caliph of Safi: and
very nice they all looked.

There is one point of Moorish manners you must never
forget. No really refined guest eats quietly. Smack your
lips and chew noisily. When, later, you are drinking tea,
let it sound as much like bath-water running down the
waste-pipe as you can simulate. And belch (forgive me
mentioning the word, but it is *most* important), belch loud
and long, like the Horn of Roland, and at each trumpeting
exclaim "Thank God!" in a heartfelt voice. For if you
neglect all this you will be taken for a very ill-bred person
indeed; and no one likes that.

All the time you are eating, the probability is you have
never seen your host—the servants have simply been put
at your disposal. And indeed you are quite likely to leave
his house without once setting eyes on him (though you
may be pretty sure he has set eyes on you!). This is part of
the theory of Arab hospitality: that you should treat the
house and servants as your own, without any bothersome
host to embarrass you; and a rather pretty theory it is.

But after you have eaten he will probably pay you a call, and drink tea with you.

Tea is the most salient feature of native Morocco. It is the universal drink of Kaid, Pasha, Caliph, Sheikh, and peasant. After you have worn your throat out with a morning's heated bargaining in the Souk, likely as not the shopkeeper will call a truce and you will refresh yourselves with tea together before starting again. It is green tea with mint added, and quantities of sugar—almost a saturated solution: a beverage much too sweet for the liking of the average tourist, but try it during a time of severe exertion and you will swear by it. On the road, it will probably be your sole form of sustenance: for the Arab works on the camel-principle—enormous feasts when he gets the chance, with long fasts between. (Indeed, the first physical necessity for a traveller in Arab countries is an elastic abdominal wall.)

It is dangerous in Morocco to drink water raw, and alcohol is rare beyond the wildest dreams of Volstead: the coffee tastes like mud (I wish they would institute an annual pilgrimage to *Mocha*): and tea it is you drink, morning noon and night.

Try the brew on your next summer hike—if you happen to have a Moor handy to show you how to do it.

Your host then arrives, and you greet each other with formal elaboration—a running fire of enquiries after the health of every person or thing connected with each other, and a running fire of "All right, thank you; all right, God be praised; all right . . ." in reply: a hand-shaking, after which you kiss the tips of your own fingers (since they have had the honour of touching your new friend's), and lay them on your heart: and a more humble kissing of the Great Man's robe on the part of your soldier. Then tea is made with an even more elaborate ritual, and drunk with what can only be described (far too mildly) as *gusto*; and after the third cup has been drunk, and a little desultory conversation attempted, and you have been given the once-over with an

intensity which will imprint you on your host's retina for
life, he leaves you for the night. Outside, the merry cackle
of your mule-boys subsides, as they curl up on the steps
under the stars, nuzzling into each other like a litter of
puppies to mitigate the frost, their stomachs cheered with
the leavings of your feast. Inside, Ali— your guide, servant,
soldier, and friend—stretches himself across the threshold,
his dagger ready under his pillow: so wrap your warm
camel's hair cloak round you, and draw the hood over
your ears, and curl up among the cushions: and it will be
dawn and time to be off almost before your head has
touched the pillow.

Time to be off on another day's mule-back jig-jog along
precipitous paths, with another night's lodging to be
blarneyed for at the end of it. And so on, and so on.

ii

But there came at last a day when something went
wrong: what it was, we never discovered for certain. We
had ridden into a valley (near the confines of the French
Protectorate) where lay the ruins of a very ancient mosque
of which wonderful accounts had reached us, and on which
we had set our hearts. We must have been only a few
hundred yards from our goal when the Caliph who ruled
there sent us a message that we must leave that part of the
country at once.

There may have been many reasons. Perhaps he was
doubtful of the behaviour of some of the more fanatical of
his subjects—I am told a French geologist was murdered
near there not very long ago—and naturally enough did
not care for the responsibility. Perhaps some French out-
post, moved by a similar anxiety, had prompted him: for
they would have fresh in their minds that murder and
kidnapping, on the part of the tribesmen, which the papers
of the whole world were full of a few months ago; and the
almost fabulous ransom which had to be paid for the

recovery of the prisoners (among whom were two little girls and the nephew of the French Resident-General). Or perhaps we had offended unwittingly in some point of ceremonial. Or perhaps he disliked our faces. Or perhaps —but there is no limit to conjecture, and anyhow the upshot was that sick with disappointment we had to turn our faces north towards Morocco and the modern world, and ride hard and ride fast if we were to reach shelter by nightfall, for it was nearly midday. The only lethal weapon we carried was a vest pocket Kodak—and even that would be useless at night!

(Moreover, the tribesmen are said to have a certain way of amusing themselves with white men they make their prisoners which would quite take the gilt off the adventure —not that we imagined it likely, if we showed elementary discretion, that we would be seriously molested.)

Sick with disappointment, and silent, we urged our mules to do their utmost back along the track through the olive groves we had ridden up so happily in the bright frosty sunlight of that same morning. On our right towered the vast snow-covered wall of the watershed; on our left, the bare crimson cliff at whose foot the river ran. Presently we forded the latter, our three boys hanging to the mules' tails and plunging manfully through the ice-cold water, and forced our mules up the slope on our left, which the noonday sun was already baking. This was in order to avoid the castle of the brother of that Caliph who had given us our congé. Then, back into the river bed, and into the dark tunnel that wound through a thick bed of reeds, and back at last to the mouth of the valley.

Here was a most curious scene. It was the junction of three tracks almost imperceptible to the eye, yet thronged with a continuous stream of traffic. On our right lay the ford; and beyond it, the path winding back over the last range of mountains to the interior of Africa. From time to time a few mules or a few camels came across: but the majority of the traffic was pedestrian—wiry little men, mostly Berbers by race, or Negroes, with thin iron shanks, barefoot, and dressed in a simple tunic, carrying a load on their shoulders or heads and keeping up hour after hour a steady swinging trot. Just as we arrived, a lady of consequence was crossing the ford, her whole head muffled in white veils till she looked like Lot's wife. Her two eunuchs were persuading her mule, by word and whip, not to indulge its evident inclination to roll her off gently into the stream. Close behind came running a cheerful-looking fellow from the Sous country, with a long silver gun over his shoulder. Ali shouted out to him in the Sous dialect to know where he was going. "Up to Morocco City to sell it to the tourists!" He flourished the gun round his head and was gone. They look primitive enough weapons, these long, fantastically decorated, muzzle-loading flintlocks; but they are surprisingly accurate. "In the Rif war," said my companion, "I saw a Riffi bring down a Spanish aeroplane with one. When we looked at the body of the pilot, the bullet had gone right through his heart!"

At the meeting of the ways was a gnarled old olive tree, and under it a little mud hut did duty as hotel, selling bread and half-rotten meat at exorbitant prices. Outside it was grouped a cavalcade of mules, loaded with bales of carpets, while the drovers took their afternoon nap; and other groups lay about somnolently in the shade. But we had no time to waste, with a disgruntled Caliph only a mile or two off: stopping only for a stirrup-cup of mint-tea, we hurried on into the mouth of a knife-cut gorge into which the river disappeared, our mules climbing from boulder to boulder like goats. It is no easy matter to keep one's seat under these circumstances: for one uses no saddle: straw panniers are flung over the mule's back (not fastened in any way) to carry his fodder and your spare luggage, and on top of this you sit, sideways as if on a sofa, drumming on his ribs with your heels. There is no grip at all, you depend entirely on balance; and when your mule is treading delicately, according to his usual preference,

along the outermost two inches of a path, your feet both
dangling over a five hundred foot drop into the river bed
beneath, and you feel your panniers beginning to slip, and
you want to scratch your back, and you meet a camel
taking the *inside* of the path with a bulging load which
seems likely to give you just that little extra push (unless
you can duck safely under it)—well, the likeness to sitting
on a sofa gets a little less obvious, somehow.

But one gets used to it surprisingly quickly, like most
things.

iii

I have a natural passion for mountains—a passion
dependent more on their shape and beauty of colour, I
admit, than their mere size, and this has led me to prefer
the tiny peaks of Wales to many far more famous ranges,
judging as I do rather by eye than by altitude-meter. But
in the Atlas there is plenty to satisfy both. Somehow, too,
the dogged sort of mood in which we rode that day, feeling
sullen and disappointed, and so quite careless of outward
fatigue or discomfort, hardly speaking except to curse our
mounts, concerned only in forcing the last possible degree
of speed out of these honest but unexcitable creatures—yet
trying to appear unhurried and unperturbed in what
practically amounted to a flight: this curious mood, I say,
gave somehow an added clearness to the eye. All that
afternoon our way lay along a narrow path halfway up
the sides of a deep, precipitous valley: sometimes descend-
ing a little to cross a *wadi*, sometimes rising a thousand feet
above the river to top a projecting bluff; a path here and
there broken away so that only a few inches remained,
here and there smothered in a landslide, where any small
misadventure would have meant precipitation into the
remote perpendicular distance: tired, angry, hot: yet the
memory which remains most clearly in my mind (and will
remain all my life, I think) was the extraordinary beauty

of all we saw. Imagine a whole world of rock and earth that is a glowing crimson in colour, bare except for a scattering of gnarled tamarisks, blazed on by an African sun: far overhead the salt-like gleam of snow-peaks, seeming to float up into the sky; down, between your feet yet far distant, a winding river as silvery as spilt mercury, with here and there a grove of olives, or a tiny village of crimson mud picked out to the eye only by its black shadows: a scene the same in kind always, yet, as the valley unwound, a perpetual changing of shape, as silhouette changed into surface, the distant grew near, the near passed abreast and vanished behind—but alas! purple passages of this sort give more pleasure to the author than the reader . . . nor do I suppose the scenery gave much pleasure to our unfortunate boys, trudging barefoot behind us for hour after hour.

They were an amusing little crew, this retinue of ours. Ali, of course, was in command of them: a tall, dark mountain-Arab, with a gentle smile and that timid expression which often graces the courage of a lion. He could not read nor write; but he knew the country like the back of his hand: and though he knew no French or English he could talk several dialects of Berber—of the utmost advantage to us, seeing that in the mountains it is only the important chiefs who know Arabic. In his snow-white robe and hood, with his black goat's-hair cloak over it and his long silver dagger on a coloured cord, he was a magnificent figure: and somehow contrived to sit even his ridiculous mule with a negligent grace. He formed part of the confidential bodyguard of one of the greatest of the Hereditary Lords of the Atlas, and his master had lent him to us for the journey with the impressive instruction that he was responsible for us with his life: a responsibility which I don't think he felt very onerous. The three boys (who were thrown in free, as makeweights so to speak, with the mules) were one Arab, one Jew, and one Negro. Of these, the Arab, Abdullah, was the least hardy. 'Abdul Aziz' we nicknamed him, in honour of a dead Sultan. He was always many miles behind us. "Where's the Sultan?" we would ask: "The sultan's dead," the others answered grinning; and then pointed back to where his ragged and forlorn figure came jog-trotting over the skyline. The joke was a simple one, but it never failed to work, time after time. As for the Jew: in Morocco a Jew, even a European one, is despised by the Arabs: he is considered streets below the Negro in social status, and is worse hated on religious grounds than the Christian, a fact which should prove interesting to Americans. Just as the Moor refuses to recognise the Gibraltarian as an Englishman, preferring to call him a Rock-scorpion, so no Jew, whatever his wealth or his Savile Row suiting, is anything but a Dog of a Yehudi.

But it was the little Negro, the smallest and wiriest of the lot, who proved both the best servant and the best companion. He did all the work, ate least, and was perpetually smiling. We asked him his name. "My name is Nothing," he replied. "Where do you come from, then?" "I am the Son of a Mule"; and 'Nothing, the Son of a Mule' he remained to us.

Your Moor cannot resist a joke, if it be simple enough. He prefers an old joke to a new one, of course; but a new joke will do, if you can make him understand it. That night we had at last, as dusk fell, reached the castle we were aiming at, only to be refused admittance by the surly Sheikh who held it. Accordingly we approached the headman of the mud village outside its walls; a dignified little Berber about four-foot-six high, with a yellow bald head and parched-up face; he was a kindly creature, and, though his master the Sheikh had forbidden him to give us shelter, he took us secretly into a little stable, swept it out, furnished it with one rush mat, and put it at our disposal. Presently the village priest came in to warn us that one of his more fanatical parishioners, hearing there were Christians in the village, intended giving trouble. Sure enough, there was soon a gigantic buck-Negro dancing up and down outside the door, inflaming his religious emotions with a tom-tom and breathing out fire and slaughter. There may be many ways of dealing with such a situation: but I certainly consider my companion's was an original one. He sprang to the door and gave his celebrated imitation of a monkey searching for fleas. The effect was electric: first astonishment amounting almost to terror; then the light of religious fervour in the man's eyes collapsed like a burst balloon, and he was soon rolling about the street helpless with laughter. So ended *that* little Holy War!

The priest and the headman stayed to take tea with us, while the village resources were taxed to provide us with supper: and a very pleasant evening we spent, somewhat a relief from the formality of baronial halls. In the shadows, but inside the door this time, squatted the Sultan and the Jew (admitted as long as we had plenty of incense to burn): but 'Nothing' we could not see.

"Where's Nothing?" I asked.

"Here's nothing!" said Abdul Aziz gravely, opening his empty hand.

"Ah, poor Negro!" said my companion, shaking his head sadly. "Negro dead!"

"Negro dead!" cried Abdullah in incredulity: "Negroes *never* die!—Look!"

He picked up the little sugar-mallet which hung on a nail and gave a resounding thump on something invisible in the dark. Immediately under the mallet appeared, suspended in air like the Cheshire Cat's, a broad white grin; and we caught the gleam of two rolling eyes. Abdullah thumped again on the woolly pate. "Negroes *can't* die!" he said disgustedly, and hung up the mallet again.

"Look at this! New-style pencil, for writing in the dark!" I said. I pulled out an ingenious little pencil with an electric bulb in the end, through which the lead passed. We blew out the candle, and I demonstrated it: the pressure of the lead on the paper completed the connection, throwing a little circle of light on the word being written: when it was lifted, the light automatically disappeared. The little Berber's breath almost died in his chest with astonishment. He tried it again and again, being able, to my surprise, to trace Arabic characters with considerable elegance. When I gave it him, I think he became my friend for life. "Don't use it too much, though," I cautioned him: "the light will get tired, and if it gets too tired, it will get ill and die." But I doubt if he would be able to keep his hands off it for long.

iv

'*He must be a dog, he goes on foot*', says the Arab proverb. I am afraid I am rather a dog by inclination, my leg-muscles lacking altogether that aristocratic flabbiness which rich Moors cultivate. Often on our journey I would have been glad to get off my meandering animal and give my legs a stretch: but it would never have done, our stock would have fallen to rock-bottom. The next day, however, our boys were thoroughly stiff after their long push of the day before: we were entering more civilised parts, more-over, where prestige was less vital; so my companion and I dismounted and put the astonished young ragamuffins on our steeds. The unfortunate Ali climbed down too, thinking it most improper to ride while we were on foot: but hardy mountaineer as he was, and able to ride day and night without fatigue, he had hardly gone on foot a hundred yards at the pace we set when his bronchial tube began to whistle and a look of approaching dissolution crept into his face. We made him, protesting, get back on his mule.

So the time went by, the last pass was crossed, and we began the long winding descent to the Plain of Marrakesh. 'Marraksh el Hamar' they call it: 'Morocco the Red': and I know of few distant views more wonderful than that of Morocco City, set in the middle of its plain with a great horse-shoe of the mountains all round it; the shell-pink city, lit up with the early morning sunlight, the tall mosque-tower of the Couta-bia—justly one of the most celebrated towers of the world—springing above the feathery surrounding palms. But that is a thing any tourist can see, in security and comfort. 'Haec inter maximas totius orbis terrarum urbes adnumerari solet', my three-hundred-year-old map tells me: now, gone is its sultanic glory: the stranger can arrive in most comfortable swift French motor-buses, and stay there in titanic hotels, and poke his gullible nose happily into its ancient markets. Marrakesh, Marrakesh, how are thy mighty fallen!

v

As we descended the mountain road we passed an ancient shrine, its little white walls and dome shadowed by its gnarled old fig-tree: and overtook an old woman who had been praying there. There was such a look of joy on her face that, inquisitive, we greeted her. She needed no asking, her story was bursting out of her.

"My name is Fatima bint Larbi, and I was a poor widow with one child, a son, living in Marrakesh. Every day I made a tray of sweetmeats and sat with them in the market-place, and so I was able to buy food for my son, though I often had none for myself. Presently from a child he grew to be a boy; and then one day he left me. For a time I could not believe that he was gone: I thought it was some boyish prank, and that he would come back. I could not bear anyone to knock at my door, for every knock I thought might be his; I used to go to the window and drive them away with curses. For many years this went on. At length I left Marrakesh and began to walk about the country, praying at every shrine I came to that the saint would find my son. One day I was praying at the shrine of Sidi Bouskri, which is above the sea, outside the city of

Safi: and when I had prayed I spoke with the priest. My name is Fatima bint Larbi, I said, and I told him my story. May Allah give you back your son! he answered. Among others praying there was a young man, and he heard what I said. Did you say you are Fatima bint Larbi, sweet-seller of Marrakesh? he asked; and when I spoke I recognised him—it was my son! So now I still walk about the country; but this time it is to give thanks for him at every shrine I come to. I am older than I was before, and as ragged, and as poor, and as hungry: but the heart within me is the heart of a Queen!"

The Fool and the Fifteen Thieves

FOR two months I had been camped in a glade of a cork-forest, in Northern Morocco. Round my tents gladioli and asphodel and marigolds grew in profusion. By night there was nothing to disturb me but the nightingales, of which there were far too many: the grouching of an occasional wild boar: the distant high piping howl of young jackals (the sort of note that bats might make if they howled). By day there was nothing to disturb me at all.

A little to the west of me, across the marshes, the Atlantic surf thundered on twenty miles of deserted sandy beach that in England we should have edged with a cement promenade and made hideous with hordes of our own bodies. In the hot middle of the day I used to ride there, in and out of the water: and swim.

I was there for no purpose at all, except that I wanted to be. I was camped in some comfort, having one large tent for use by night, and another by day, as well as cook-tents and store-tents. I had embroidered cushions and gaudy carpets, and braziers and trays and basins and ewers of polished copper and brass and silver. There was no European with me; only Arabs.

My life was supervised and arranged for me by Hamed, a kind of Oriental Jeeves, who added to the accomplishments of the English one a remarkable tenor voice, great ability as a story-teller, and handiness in the use of a knife for what the American Negro euphemistically calls 'social purposes'. This last skill had been acquired only after much practice, as two murderous scars across his own throat witnessed. He could cook like an angel: and once arranged a dinner-party for me (complete with a string quartette) at ten minutes' notice.

He handled me as a wise schoolmistress handles a child.

Then there was my groom, a slatternly urchin, who dis-liked horses and work, and who for some reason was always called Rosebud. Next was a lumpish creature, whose sole advantage was that he knew the country-side, and could conjure butter and eggs out of a palmetto clump: indeed, one day when all other supplies failed, he even fed me on locusts and wild honey. And then there was a 'Khayyám', an expert in tents, who took charge whenever the tents blew down, as they often did; and mended their tents lovingly, for they had once been hand-some tents, and were lined with brocade, and had double roofs, and windows and curtains; but they had seen fully twenty years' campaigning before they became my property. They had once belonged to the famous Kaid Sir Harry, the Scotsman who became Moorish Commander-in-Chief.

These men formed the nucleus; but I had not been established there very long before my camp became a recognised stopping-place for travellers—what few passed. Frequently I would see some complete stranger helping with the work of the camp; and, if his gifts lay that way, he would often come to my own tent after supper in the evening and sing, or play the lute, or tell long stories that were own blood-brother to those in the Arabian Nights.

But at last, as the news spread, my camp drew the attention of less desirable visitors. One night (when I happened myself to have ridden off to Tangier, and did not return till the following afternoon) marauders paid a surprise visit.

When I got back, all was confusion. Not one of my Arabs had heard the robbers arrive nor depart, for few men can sleep as soundly as a sentinel; though hoof-marks showed plainly for a short distance which way they had gone.

Their booty was miscellaneous: it consisted of one carpet, a black and red cloak of goat's hair, a brass kettle,

a snuff-box, the spare ribbon of my typewriter, and two
bananas.

No one, of course, was to blame—that was explained to
me quite infallibly: the robbers must have been as light-
foot as butterflies and as invisible as air, if one were to
believe my guardians' account of the affair. But I was
angry, I was unreasonable. I demanded that everyone
should at once set out in pursuit—though the thieves were
probably over the border by now, and my property in the
hands of receivers in Alcazar.

The night was dark and uninviting. The other Arabs
looked despairingly at Hamed for rescue; and Hamed did
not fail them.

"We will start immediately," said Hamed. Then he
added: "But all this reminds me of the story of Ish-ha and
the Fifteen Thieves: do you know that story?"

"I do not know it," said I. "Who was this Ish-ha?"

"Ish-ha," said Hamed, "was a Fool. He was the greatest
Fool that there has ever been in Morocco: that is to say he
was the greatest Fool there has ever been in the World. He
was so great a Fool that when he was a boy and his mother
told him to watch the door while she went into the market
to buy food, he lifted the door off its hinges and carried it
with him down the street to where he could play with the
other boys without ceasing to watch it . . . He was such a
Fool that one day, when he was sitting on the bough of a
tree, he began to saw it off between the trunk and himself.
Presently a man came by and said: 'You will fall, Ish-ha.'
So Ish-ha finished sawing off the bough and fell to the
ground with it: then he ran after the man who had told
him he would fall, crying out that he must be a great
prophet, an unparalleled seer in foretelling the future, to
have prophesied so unerringly that he was about to fall,
simply through seeing him sitting on a bough and sawing
it off . . . He was so great a Fool that the Sultan had him to
live at his Court and would often give him large sums in
reward for his most unparalleled acts of folly. He was such

a Fool that when he died a whole quarter of the city was named after him, that folly like his might never be forgotten."

"But the story of Ish-ha and the Fifteen Thieves," I interrupted, "is it a long one?"

"By no means," said Hamed. "It will only take a few minutes to tell. It will hardly delay us at all: then we will set out in pursuit of the robbers, and, if Allah wills it, we shall overtake them. But if Allah does not will it we should not have overtaken them even if we had started out two hours ago."

"Very well, Hamed," I said, "tell me the story."

I leant back comfortably on my cushions, and Hamed expediently lit and handed to me the *kif*-pipe, the further to soothe my temper. Then, squatting on his heels in front of me, with all the cunning of a Scheherezade in his soul, he began the tale.

*

"In the time of Ish-ha the Fool," began Hamed, "there were in the city of Fez fifteen brothers who were thieves. At night they would separate, and each would rob a different house; and in the morning they would meet at a certain café in a poor quarter of the city of Fez; and there they would divide their spoils, and tell each other the stories of their adventures.

"Now, one night one of the robbers came to the house of Ish-ha the Fool: and just because the master of the house was known far and wide as the greatest fool in the Kingdom, the robber thought he had no need to be quiet about his work. Having forced the front door, he bumped and banged about as carelessly as if he were in his own home.

"But, in an inner room, Ish-ha was in bed with his wife; and when she heard the front door forced she woke him up.

"'Get up, Ish-ha,' she said; 'there is a burglar in the house.'

"But Ish-ha only grunted, and told her not to disturb him. Presently she heard the burglar upset a pile of dishes in the kitchen with a great clatter; so she woke Ish-ha again.

"'Get up!' she said. 'There is a burglar, and he is carrying off everything we possess!'

"'Don't disturb me, woman!' said Ish-ha in a loud voice, so that the burglar could hear; 'if there is a thief here, what does it matter? I have put all my money in a leather bag and hidden it at the bottom of the well in the kitchen. He will never think of looking for it there.'

"So, when the burglar heard that, he stripped off all his clothes and climbed down into the well. Then Ish-ha slipped quietly out, took away the burglar's clothes, and then got back into bed.

"There was no leather bag at the bottom of the well, and the water was cold; and when the burglar came up again his clothes were gone. He knew very well that Ish-ha must have taken them; so he waited, shivering, till Ish-ha should go to sleep again, that he might creep into the inner room and recover them. But Ish-ha now was full of wakefulness, and every time the thief tried the handle of the inner door Ish-ha coughed, as much as to say, '*I am awake: I hear you!*'

"So this went on till nearly dawn, and the thief despaired of recovering his clothes. If he were not to be found wandering naked in the streets of Fez by day, he must depart at once: and this he finally determined to do. But as he was going out Ish-ha heard him, and called out to him in a loud voice, 'Shut the front door after you, if you please, Mr Thief!'

"The thief answered angrily, 'If you get a new suit of clothes from everyone who tries to burgle your house, Ish-ha, I should think that you would rather I left it open!'

"With that, the thief departed, and went to the café

which was the rendezvous of his brothers, and told them of the cruel trick which had been played upon him. Then they were all filled with indignation, and swore that they would have their revenge upon the Fool.

"So the next night, instead of separating as usual, and each going to a separate house, all fifteen of them came to the house of Ish-ha. They forced open the door and ransacked the whole house (except of course his bedroom).

"'Wake up!' said his wife: 'the house is full of thieves!'

"But Ish-ha only grunted and said, 'Peace, woman! Let me go to sleep.' And he began to snore as loudly as he could.

"Meanwhile, the thieves took out of the house everything there was in it. They carried off the carpets and the mirrors, the censers and the braziers, the cushions and the wall-hangings and the curtains: they did not leave so much as one earthenware pot in the kitchen.

"'Get up! Get up!' cried Ish-ha's wife angrily: 'if you were a *man* you wouldn't lie in bed like this, while robbers took away everything you possess!'

"'Peace, woman!' said Ish-ha.

"At last the burglars had carried everything into the street, and were about to depart, when suddenly Ish-ha leapt out of bed, and crying 'By Allah! here is something they have forgotten!' he caught hold of the mattress on which he and his wife were lying—upset her on to the floor —put the mattress on his head—and ran out into the street after the thieves.

"Now the night was dark; and since there were already fifteen thieves, each with a burden on his head, they were not likely to notice that there were now sixteen of them: and Ish-ha's face was covered by the mattress he was carrying. So Ish-ha went along with the thieves, until presently they met the Night Patrol of the city watchmen.

"Now the thieves, who looked like respectable porters, were about to go by; but Ish-ha went and addressed himself to the captain of the Patrol:

"'I am a foreign merchant,' said Ish-ha, 'who has just taken a house in this town; and I engaged these men to help me move into it, but they are so lazy that night fell and the work was not yet finished. Now they are afraid to carry all these valuables in the streets at night: they fear lest robbers should set on them, and so they have begged me, noble Captain, that I should ask you to come with us as escort, to see that no one should attack us.'

"When he said this the robbers were astonished; but naturally they did not dare say anything.

"'Certainly,' said the Captain of the Guard; 'we will come with you. The streets are not half as safe as they should be. Where do you live?'

"So Ish-ha gave him his address; and the unfortunate thieves had to turn round and carry everything back to the house from which they had taken it. When they arrived there Ish-ha ordered them about in a most imperious fashion, making them put back everything exactly as they had found it, at the same time detaining the Captain of the watchmen with his conversation. Only when everything was in its place did Ish-ha let the fifteen thieves depart; and even then, as they went, he shouted after them: 'Now remember, you lazy porters, that when I hired you this morning I paid you fully in advance, so it is no good coming back to me tomorrow and demanding a tip for what you have done!'"

*

Now the story as Hamed told it was not as short and as bald as this: it was embellished with a wealth of detail that would have filled an ordinary-sized novel. The Arab story-teller excels at this long spinning-out of detail: he will begin the morning with a description of the hero's bridle as he starts out on a journey, and by the afternoon be still describing the horse's tail. There was little in this narrative that Hamed left to the imagination—the colour of the beard of the fifteenth thief, the embroidery on the smallest cushion that they carried off—if I were to repeat one-tenth of his descriptions I should keep you, as he kept me, till long past midnight.

As he finished, the moon was sinking over the marshes towards the Atlantic, and the tall candle in the brass candle-stick by the tent door, guttering in the breeze, had burnt to a stump; but by its light I could still see the gleam of the fascinated eyes of the other Arabs, as they squatted listening, in a half-circle outside. Hamed bent forward and blew to life the charcoal in the little earthen brazier in front of me, then put a few pieces of native incense on it so that soon the tent was filled by its fascinating and nostalgic scent.

It was too late now for any pursuit of robbers through the inky bush, where djinns and devils—let alone the Father of Tushes himself, the wild boar—may lurk for the unwary: and so we all went to sleep.

I never saw my missing possessions again; but then I do not suppose I should have, even if I had sent them off in pursuit as I meant to. It was not the will of Allah.

And I should, moreover, have missed the story of the Fool and the Fifteen Thieves.

Two Pots of Gold

I WAS digging a well, last March, in my garden in
Morocco, and building a roof on the kitchen. I em-
ployed for the work a master-mason called Mulay Ali, an
Arab with some Negro blood, aged about fifty: and Mulay
Ali employed two very old women and a boy.

They divided their labour like this: while the two old
women and the boy carried stone in the hot sun, it was
usual for Mulay Ali to seat himself in the shade of my great
fig-tree, for two hours each morning or sometimes three, in
order to discuss without precipitancy what I should pay
him for that day's parcel of work.

For some weeks, this was the regular custom. But one
morning, without sending any message, Mulay Ali did not
arrive at all; and the next, though he came, he seemed far
from being himself. It was plain that something had shaken
him badly. His arguments that day were palpably weak,
his rhetoric lacked force, his lying sounded tinny, a mere
matter of form. To my great astonishment he finally
agreed to a reasonable price in less than half an hour.

Mulay Ali, it was plain, had something serious on his
mind; and, the bargain once struck, he began to pour it
out without further preamble.

Had I myself ever seen a Djinn, he asked. Or known
those who had dealings with them?

I looked at him in some surprise: one hardly expects
such Arabian-Nights-stuff from one's builder, even in
Morocco. But he was plainly too much in earnest to have
the least fear of my ridiculing him.

No, I had never seen a Djinn. But I remembered how an
old white donkey had scared the life out of me the night
before, when I was crossing the Arab cemetery in the dark
on my way to Edward Wolfe's house ... Presumably

43

Mulay Ali had had some trivial scare of this sort. Nevertheless, I encouraged him to go on. And I was glad I did: for it was a strange rigmarole he had to tell: an unlikely sort of tale for the year 1932.

*

"There is a poor woman living in such-and-such a quarter of the town," began Mulay Ali, passing me his *kif*-pipe for a friendly puff. "Until recently, she shared a tiny house there with her old father. Now, though these two lived together in a very poor way, so that the woman had to carry water for folk from the public fountains in order to buy food for them both, her father often hinted to her that there was treasure hidden in the courtyard of their little dwelling. Before his time came to die, he said, he would reveal to her where it was buried.

"All this was common knowledge in the quarter.

"Now, last week the old man fell suddenly dead in the market-place, and his lips were closed before ever he could tell his daughter the secret. He was buried, as our custom is, before sunset; but even before his body had been washed, and the grave-clothes laid out ready to wind him, the creditors had begun to gather round. For they had all heard of the treasure; and if Fatima could not find it at once, they could seize the house on account of their debts; and so they hoped to get possession of the buried treasure themselves.

"Now, there was a certain man from the Sous lodging in the same street as Fatima's house. Some considered him a Holy Man, on account of the number of prayers he said; but his holiness was by no means beyond question, since it was also said he practised spells and charms, which is forbidden to a good Moslem. Certain small miracles he was known to have done; but whether with the help of Allah, or of the Powers of Darkness—of Djinns and Afrits —the town could not decide.

"To him, at any rate, Fatima went for help, the day after the funeral, and told him what had happened. 'That is easy,' he said: 'if Allah wills, I shall find the gold with no trouble at all. I will come tomorrow before noon; so see that you have a mason there, in readiness to dig wherever my prayers discover the gold to be.'

"So then Fatima came to me," continued Mulay Ali, "and arranged that I should be on hand. I knew that Soussi well: we met outside in the alley-way, and arrived at the house together. There we found Fatima and her two brothers, whom she had invited to see that she was not cheated in any way. When we were all inside, we carefully locked the door of the house, so that no one could go in or out, and sat in the courtyard.

"First, the Soussi asked for a little brazier of charcoal; and, having seen that it was well alight, had it put on one side and attended to 'until he should need it'. Then he began to pray, and we all recited the scriptures of our religion out loud with him for many hours till we were very weary. But nothing happened. So at length he took from his pouch some sheets of paper with strange writings on them, and shuffled them three times, and then studied them carefully, still praying the while. We sat there, expecting something strange to happen, but nothing that appeared very uncommon took place: only the Soussi suddenly rose up, and making for a certain spot in the courtyard, said to me: *'Dig there!'*

"So there I dug. I found that there was an old disused conduit, built by the Portuguese long ago, which passed under the courtyard at this point; and sure enough, when I was able to remove part of the masonry of it, I drew out two earthenware pots! These the woman and her brothers broke in a great hurry. They were filled with gold.

"At this Fatima was delighted, and was on the point of making handsome presents to the Soussi and to myself, and dismissing us; but that Son of the Unnameable stopped her. 'So far,' he said, 'we have only two little pots of gold.

Who knows what other treasures may be hidden elsewhere in the house? A king's ransom, perhaps? Remain seated, and keep silence: I have more to do.'

"This time he did not pray to Allah, but instead he muttered strange words in the Shleuh tongue that they all talk in the Sous, and called for the glowing brazier, and threw on it some powder he had in his pouch. We were much shocked, for it was plain he was doing something contrary to the True Religion. And indeed he was: for a great cloud of smoke rose up—and, by Allah, before the eyes of all of us that sat there in the house, that cloud of smoke took on it the living shape of a Djinn!

"At this we were much frightened—and we were none of us children, or fools. 'It is now necessary,' said the magician to Fatima, 'if we are to go on with this business without danger, that you should tell the Djinn you approve beforehand of everything I may bid him do.'

"Fatima was so terrified by this that she could hardly speak; but she was just able to form the necessary words with her lips. Whereupon the magician rose to his feet, and calling to the Djinn said: 'Take up that gold!'

"So the Djinn took it, and held it in his hands.

"'Now', said the sorcerer to the Djinn, 'take up me also!' So the Djinn lifted him in his arms.

"Then he cried out in a great loud voice, 'Son of Eblis! She has given her consent to whatever I command you! *Away to the Sous!*'

"There was a clap of thunder, and the ground yawned at our feet, so that we all thought that we were dead; and it was some little time before we found that we were not. But the Djinn was gone; and, what is more, the magician and the gold were gone with him: nothing remained of the treasure we had found, but the hole in the ground and the two broken pots. Not one single piece of gold had been left in the earth—though we scratched like hens for it, and wore our fingers sore.

"At that, the two brothers cried out against Fatima for

a great fool, in giving her consent beforehand to whatever the Djinn should do; but truly at the time we were *all* so terrified, I doubt if any of us would have been wiser.

"Yet we were all equally incensed with the wickedness of the cheating magician, and after some talk went all together to complain to the Cadi.

"The Cadi agreed that the magician had done a very wicked thing; but there was little which *he* could do, he said. The woman having given her consent beforehand, the magician was legally within his rights. Then the Cadi turned his face away from us and talked of other things, and we left him.

"So then we went to the Christian police, and told our story to that Dutch Officer who is in charge there; but he also could be of no help. 'We International police,' he said, 'are only allowed to catch criminals within the International Zone itself. But, by your story, this wicked magician and the Djinn are now six hundred miles away, in the Valley of the Sous—which is under French jurisdiction. For Djinns,' he went on, 'travel (like the telegraph) in the twinkling of an eye: which is much faster than any of my policemen can travel.'

"So then we went from there to the Mendoubia (the government offices), and demanded to see the Sultan's Viceroy, still hoping to get justice for the poor woman. But the Viceroy himself refused to see us; and it was late evening before it could be decided to which department our complaint ought properly to be addressed. At last, however, as we refused to go away unsatisfied, they sent us to the Passport Office.

"There they looked in a book, and told us the number of the magician's passport; they even showed us a print of his finger. They promised to send a telegram to the frontier, with the number of the passport written plainly in it, for all to know: 'And so,' they said, 'we shall certainly catch him, as soon as he tries to cross.'

"But Djinns, as the Dutch Officer had said, travel in the

twinkling of an eye; and this one had a long start. They travel, too, invisibly, or in the strangest disguises. A Djinn can carry a camel through a keyhole: or hide himself in the smoke curling from your own cigarette. We knew well in our hearts that before ever the thunder had emptied itself out of our ears, that magician would have been safe with the gold in his own village. How then could the Christian soldiers stop him at the frontier? And yet . . . even this is possible to Allah, to whom alone homage is due."

*

Mulay Ali finished his story, and paused. Overhead the mailplane droned on its daily journey to Casablanca. Beneath me in a street of the lower town, I could just see a tourist in a bowler hat, balanced unhappily on a reeling donkey. Perhaps that bobbing bowler reminded me of a mooring-buoy, jerked from side to side in a tide race . . . at any rate, I found myself fixing my regard on it, as if it were a symbol of security in fantastic seas. Djinns, passports, and magicians indeed! What rubbish!

As if he shared something of my mood, Mulay Ali dragged me off to inspect the progress on my kitchen roof. "You will notice," he said proudly, "that we Moslem master-workers do not now make roofs as our forefathers used to, by laying sticks across, and covering them with earth. The method we have recently invented is called 'reinforced concrete'; and it is so strong, so infinitely superior to the old method that I am told even Christian builders in Europe are beginning to use it also."

Reinforced concrete . . . Djinns and Afrits . . . "Mulay Ali," I said firmly, "take me to the house of this Fatima!"

Before we arrived at her little hovel, the row there could be heard a hundred yards off. Fatima, a powerful-looking young woman, stood in the doorway, her head and face entirely covered in bath-towels for decency, her brown

arms and legs cleared for action, while her strident voice
rose high above the squawking and babbling of the group
of native Jews—creditors evidently—whose entrance she
was forbidding.

Mulay Ali shouldered a way for us through this crowd,
and we were soon in the little courtyard. I noticed the
magician's slippers still standing neatly side by side where
he had taken them off before beginning to read the Koran.
Fatima bolted the door on her creditors, and without the
slightest change of expression began to screech for my aid
in catching the wicked magician.

I looked about me. Truly the ground had yawned at
their feet! All that part of the town is built actually on top
of ancient ruins—granaries, powder-magazines, cisterns
and what-not, that the English blew up when they evacuated the town in the seventeenth century. Half the courtyard—disturbed perhaps by the operation of Mulay Ali's
pick during the gold-hunt—had collapsed into some sub-
terranean vault of this kind.

But surely the magician had not escaped that way. I
shone my flash-lamp into the farthest corners of the vault;
and then, sticking out of the rubble, I saw something that
was quite plainly a big toe . . .

It was a gruesome business digging out the unfortunate
necromancer, and I did not wait to see it done. So I never
discovered whether she found her two pots of gold under
his thieving body.

Likely she didn't. For I happened to know something of
Fatima's two pious brothers, that she had called in to see
fair play. Likely enough one of them had taken advantage
of the smoke and confusion when the courtyard collapsed
to tip up the magician's heels and vanish the treasure into
his own capacious satchel. In that case, Fatima might
whistle for it.

The Will

THERE was once a man who had three sons and a fair property, and the will he made was a strange one. All his property, he said, should go to that son who should prove himself the laziest.

Now all three sons were lazy. Indeed they were a by-word in the city for their laziness; but which was the laziest of the three it seemed hard to say. They argued the point amongst themselves with great anger, and at length agreed to go before the Cadi.

The Cadi listened to the terms of the suit, and then addressing the eldest brother he said to him:

"Tell me, how lazy are you?"

Then the eldest brother rose and prostrated himself before the Cadi and said:

"This very morning I was sitting by the well and a cup stood on the rim of the well and I was consumed with thirst, but I sat there for an hour and waited until my mother came and dipped herself a cup full of water to drink. Then I said to my mother: 'For shame, to leave your son here thirsty! Give me to drink what water is left in the cup.'"

Then the Cadi asked the same question of the second brother, and he, too, rose and came before the Cadi.

"Last night," he said, "my mother said to me: 'Shut the street door and let us go to bed.' But I thought to myself, 'Every night people close their street doors and go to bed, only to rise up again in the morning to open them! What a waste of time!' So I listened not to my mother's words, but sat where I was and spent the night there, and left the door wide."

Then the Cadi asked the third brother, who sat at the back of the Court:

"Tell me," he said, "how lazy are you?"

But the third brother simply sat where he was and muttered something. The Cadi repeated his question, and again the third brother muttered in a low voice.

"Tell me," said the Cadi to one of the bystanders, "what he says."

"He says," replied the bystander, "that if you will come down here into the back of the Court, he will tell you; but to get up from where he is sitting and come to you is far too much trouble."

"This case," said the Cadi, "is easily decided, I think." And he awarded the whole property to the third brother.

The Effects of Hashish

THOSE who are in the habit of taking hashish frequently do remarkably foolish things, although their lives, perhaps, may be happy ones.

Two women, who were friends, and both happened to be married to takers of hashish, were bemoaning their fate to each other; each saying that her own husband was the more foolish in his actions of the two. At last one of them said:

"I can prove it. Come to my house tomorrow and see what I will make my husband do."

So next day in the presence of her friend she took an earthenware pot, such as ordinarily contains millet, and filled it with water, and covered it over; then she woke her husband where he was sleeping comfortably in a corner and told him to take it to the miller and get it ground. Now millers in Morocco are all Jews. So her husband carried the pot of water to the nearest miller and gave it him and said: "Grind this into meal for me quickly," and promptly fell asleep again in the corner.

When the Jewish miller saw that what he had been given was a pot of water, he guessed that he had to deal with a taker of hashish; so he got a razor and cut off the sleeping man's beard, and taking off from his head the red fez such as all Mohammedans wear, he replaced it with his own black Jewish cap. Then he woke him, saying the meal was now ground.

Back home the man went, and knocked at his door; and when his wife opened it at first she did not recognise him.

"What do you want?" she said.

"What do I want!" he answered. "Isn't this my house? Aren't you my wife? Haven't I been to the miller to get some millet ground?"

"You!" said his wife, who could now hardly stop herself from laughing. "*This* your house! You dirty Jew! *Me* your wife?"

He looked at her in amazement; whereupon she seized a mirror and thrust it into his hands. First he stared at his own face in astonishment and then he cried out:

"Ah! Now I understand. You are quite right—the dirty Jew! he has left *me* sleeping in his shop, and come here himself instead of me!"

And if she had not stopped him, he would have run back down the street.

"Allah!" she exclaimed to her friend, "could a man do anything more foolish than that!"

"You are quite right," replied her friend: "you win!"

The Country Parson

WITH the mosques in a small country village it is not as it is with the mosques in a town: there is often no regular priest attached to them at all, and no regular services. Fakihs wander about the country with their Korans in a bag over their shoulders, and when they come to a village where there is no priest they bargain with the villagers to remain and lead the prayers for a year. At the end of that time, if parson and parishioners agree well together, they may stay on; but if not—if the parson has not been fed to his liking, for instance—he moves on elsewhere. Often these vagabond Fakihs are only half-educated fellows and know very little of their job; while the villagers can neither understand the Koran nor perform, themselves, the simplest act of worship.

There was a certain Fakih who spent a year in a small village in the mountains; and *he* had not even a whole Koran; he had lost all but the first two chapters! Therefore, instead of reading as he should gradually from one end of the Koran to the other, he only read these first two chapters over and over again. Now when he came to the end he was in the habit of repeating the following words: 'Dora Brigador'. By these words he meant, 'Now we will begin again': but they are not Arabic nor any language I have ever heard of. They came out of his own head.

At the end of his year he passed on, and another more learned Fakih took his place. Now this new Fakih read the Koran right through in the proper manner, of course; and his parishioners noted with surprise that he left out these two strange words 'Dora Brigador', with which they had grown familiar.

This troubled them, and they came to him in a body. "How is it," they said, "that you do not say 'Dora

Brigador', like our former Fakih used to?" The new Fakih repeated the meaningless words to himself, and said he had never heard of them; that certainly they were not in the Koran, and if the late Fakih was in the habit of using them he was an ignorant fellow and no true Fakih at all. Thus the village was divided into two parties; some upheld the late Fakih, and some the new.

Now it happened that some of the villagers, going to a distant market, met their late Fakih and told him what had happened, and how the new Fakih said that he was an impostor. To this the late Fakih replied that the new one was an impostor. "See," he said: "on this piece of paper I will write a few words in the purest Arabic; if he can read them he is a learned man, even as I am; but if he can't, he is an ignorant fool!"

He then wrote upon the paper: '*I can read one word, but not the rest.*'

When the villagers got home, they told the other parishioners of their meeting with their late Fakih, and showed them the paper; whereupon they all decided to go in a body to the new Fakih and put him to the test.

"Since none of us can read," they said, "we want you to tell us what is written on this piece of paper."

The Fakih read: '*I can read one word, but not the rest.*'

"What!" they cried: "you call yourself a learned man, and you can only read one word out of the whole sentence?" And, too stupid to understand his explanations, they drove him with buffets from the village.

*

The Fakih then went on to another village, and there the people were even more ignorant than at the first one. Every Friday he led the prayers in the Mosque; but he led them alone, for no one attended; nor did the villagers pray privately, as they should, nor perform their ablutions, nor any other of the rites of Islam. At this he was much shocked, and he called them together and chid them.

"How is it," he said, "you call yourselves Moslems, but you neither pray nor do anything else that Moslems should?"

"Forgive us," said the villagers: "it is our ignorance. We have had no one to teach us: how should we know?"

"Then I will teach you," said the Fakih.

So, on Friday, they all came to the Mosque.

"Do as I do," said the Fakih, "and say what I say."

He then took his stand, facing towards Mecca; and the people stood behind him, and he began to pray.

"Allah Akbar!" he intoned (God is Almighty!), bowing low; and the congregation behind him intoned "Allah Akbar!" and bowed also.

"Allah Akbar!" he said a second time, kneeling down and touching the floor with his forehead.

Now the floor of this Mosque was made of large loose planks; and the movements of the man behind the Fakih shifted one of these slightly, so that the Fakih's nose was caught between that plank and the rest.

"Almighty God!" said the Fakih for the third time; and then added in a lower voice, "shift your knees, for my nose is caught between the planks."

"Almighty God!" intoned the whole congregation, "shift your knees, for my nose is caught between the planks."

"Fool!" said the Fakih: "it is mine alone that is caught!"

"Fool!" repeated the whole congregation: "it is mine alone that is caught!"

Thereupon the Fakih upped with his heel, and kicked the man behind him under the chin so as to get his nose released. Whereupon the congregation, determined to follow their priest in all things, each religiously kicked the one behind under the chin. But the Fakih arose, full of wrath; and putting his Koran into his sack, he swung it over his shoulder and set off again on his travels: though, after all, it was not the villagers' fault.

The Red Lantern

THERE was once a poor sweet-seller in the city of Marrakesh, and every day he grew poorer. Why this was I do not know: but at last a time came when he could no longer buy honey with which to make his sweets. When that time came he was ashamed to become a beggar, so he said to himself:

"I will leave Marrakesh and cross the mountains, and perhaps in some other country I may meet with better fortune."

Now no man likes to travel into a new land penniless and altogether without possessions: so Ahmed, the poor sweet-seller, set out on his travels bearing all that he owned in the world. This burden, however, was not heavy; for it was a small lantern made of tin and set with red glass.

For many days Ahmed journeyed across the mountains subsisting upon the hospitality of the natives (which was meagre); and at last he came to a broad and prosperous valley, with a great city set in it of which no traveller had ever told him. So Ahmed approached the gates of the city and spoke with some men that he found there. Great was their astonishment to find he was a stranger; for no strangers, it seemed, ever visited that city. They took him to the Pasha; and the Pasha made him a guest in his own house, which was the richest Ahmed had ever seen or heard of, far richer than anything in Marrakesh. Jewels lay about in heaps, gold was used for every menial purpose. There, for the three days required by the Law of the Prophet, the Pasha used Ahmed with the greatest kindness. But then came the time for Ahmed to depart. At this Ahmed was very troubled; for he could not, he felt, leave such a kind host without making him a present, and the only thing he had to give was his trumpery little lantern of tin and red glass. Still, he hoped that the Pasha would realise that this was all he possessed, and accept the gift in the spirit in which it was given; so before taking his departure he presented the lantern to the Pasha.

The Pasha took the lantern and examined it with wonder and delight: for it is a curious thing, but in that city there was *no* glass! Glass, indeed, had never been heard of; and to see the light of a candle shining at him through red glass was a wonderful and miraculous sight to that Pasha. Delighted as he was with the lantern, however, the receipt of it made him uncomfortable in his turn. One could not receive so valuable a gift as that without oneself giving some present of great worth; and how he was able to give a present of equal value he did not know, for he had nothing in his Treasuries but a lot of common gold, a ton or two of the usual rubies, a room full of the most ordinary emeralds, and some chests of diamonds that no one would look at twice. How could he possibly, therefore, make to the stranger a fitting return for his gift?

The only thing, he concluded, was to give that which he had: to give Ahmed twelve camel-loads of gold and jewels, and trust—worthless as the present was—that Ahmed would accept it in the spirit in which it was given. So this he did: and Ahmed drove his twelve camels back safe over the mountains to Marrakesh.

Arrived at Marrakesh, Ahmed bought himself a beautiful garden full of palm trees and oranges, of jasmine and scented lemon; a garden never quiet because of the running of water and the voices of nightingales; and built himself there a palace of the finest marble, and lived in it as a rich and happy man.

Now Ahmed had a brother named Said, a small shop-keeper who had grown well-to-do as Ahmed became poor, but, instead of helping Ahmed, was at last unwilling even to acknowledge him as his brother. But now that Ahmed was wealthy, this brotherly relationship which existed between them suddenly recurred to Said's memory, and he called upon Ahmed, and talked to him in a very loving and brotherly manner; and Ahmed entertained him comfortably and made him rich presents.

But in all that visit Said failed to discover whence it was that his brother's wealth had come.

So at last he asked his brother outright: and Ahmed, who was a simple person with no jealousy for anybody, told him the story exactly as it had happened. *Why* it had happened like that still puzzled him: he could not understand why the Pasha had made him such rich presents, since it had not occurred to him that the lantern had seemed to the Pasha a thing of value: but, since the Pasha *had* made the presents, he accepted what God had sent and did not worry very much about it.

Now when Said heard this story he was even more astonished than his brother had been, and could not give up thinking about it day or night. At last he argued it out to himself like this:

"What has happened to my brother might happen to myself: and if they gave my brother all that wealth in exchange for a trumpery red glass lantern, what might they not give me in exchange for a present of real value?"

Whereupon Said went to his shop, and bought mules, and packed upon their backs all the merchandise he possessed; and sold his house, and with the money bought more merchandise, and packed that also upon the mules, and set out into the mountains by the route that his brother told him.

Now, when Ahmed had gone into those mountains he had been protected by the sure shield of his poverty; and coming back with his camel-loads of treasure he had been protected by the special will of Allah: for those mountains are the abode of robbers, and no worse robbers exist between the four corners of the earth. Hardly had Said gone more than five days' journey from Marrakesh when these robbers set upon him, and took away his mules, and beat him, and left him almost dead under an argan tree:

and when he recovered his senses, Said found himself as poor now as his brother Ahmed had once been. But shame and fear of the robbers prevented him from turning back; so he hastened on as fast as his wounds would allow him, and at last came to the broad and fertile valley, even as his brother had done.

Arrived at the city, he was treated as hospitably as his brother had been, and was taken to the Pasha's house, and his wounds anointed; and he was fed, and treated with every kindness, for three days. But then the time came for him too to leave: and now he bitterly regretted the loss of all those magnificent presents with which he had started out to give the Pasha. Nothing of his possessions remained but his watch; an old brass watch of a very ordinary kind. Well, it was all he had: and his brother, after all, had but given a tin lantern: so he would try his luck. And he presented the watch to the Pasha.

Now in this he was very fortunate, that watches (like glass) had never been heard of in that city; and the Pasha, therefore, valued this watch far above the wealth of all those mule-loads of merchandise which the robbers had seized! He valued it so greatly that he racked his brains to think of some adequate return to make for it: some treasure which he could give to Said which would not leave him *too* shamefully the stranger's debtor. Of gold and jewels he had plenty; but what were gold and jewels in return for such a gift? . . . Only one treasure had he in his Treasury fit to exchange for that watch: that treasure, the most valued thing he had, which the other stranger had given him—the red lantern.

Thus, with infinite regret and great ceremony, Ahmed's red glass lantern was brought out from the velvet cushion where it rested in the strongest room of the whole Treasury, and presented to Said. And with that guerdon of his travels, Said set out back to the city of Marrakesh whence he had come: and you may imagine that on this return journey the robbers found no occasion to trouble him.

The Canary

Nᴏᴛ long ago—not more than two or three generations
—there lived a famous Wit in the town of Tangier,
whose name was Si Haman a-Filal; and for him the Pasha
of those days created a special office, making him Supreme
Judge of all Trumpery Causes.

Now there was a small cobbler in Tangier at that time
with a shop near the gate of the Water-port. He had in his
shop a little canary-bird in a cage. One day as he was sitting
cobbling shoes an old Pilgrim came by, who was fascinated
by the song of the bird. For fully an hour he stood and
stared at it, with his eyes open and his mouth open,
blocking the light from the cobbler's shop; and he then
began to beseech the cobbler to sell it to him. This the
cobbler was unwilling to do, as he was fond of the bird;
but the Pilgrim became such a nuisance, returning day
after day and using every kind of persuasion, that at last
the cobbler said he would sell the bird for twenty dollars.

Now the Pilgrim was poor, and twenty dollars is a high
price for a canary-bird; yet in less than an hour the
Pilgrim was back with the money, and had bought the
bird, and departed with it for good (so the cobbler hoped).

Three days passed; and back came the Pilgrim with the
bird.

"Give me back my twenty dollars," he said, "and take
your bird."

At that the cobbler grew very angry.

"I did not want to sell it to you," he said; "it was you
who insisted on buying it; and now you come back and
worry me again! What right have you to do this?"

"The bird won't sing," said the Pilgrim. "Ever since I
took it home it sits in its cage, and though now and again
it says 'Twit! Twit!' not a song have I had out of it."

"I don't care," said the cobbler, "that is your own fault. There was no stipulation in our bargain that the bird should sing; and I repeat that I did not want to sell it to you but you insisted on buying it, so now be off with you."

At that the Pilgrim began to raise a great clamour, and all the bystanders collected and wanted to know what the trouble was. So then both parties told them their story; and partly because the Pilgrim was so old, and partly because he seemed so furious, and partly because good Moslems have anyhow a weakness for a holy man who has made the Pilgrimage to Mecca, they took his part against the cobbler.

"Have you no shame?" they said. "Give this poor man back his twenty dollars, and take your bird."

So, to be quit of the matter, the cobbler did this. He gave the Pilgrim his twenty dollars and hoped he would then depart.

"Wait a bit," said the Pilgrim. "I have fed this worthless bird of yours for three days. It is only fair you should refund me the value of the three days' canary-seed that it has eaten."

At that the cobbler became furious beyond words. Out of sheer kindness, he said, he had rescinded the bargain— and now the old man expected him to refund the cost of three days' canary-seed, a debt for which there is hardly a small enough coin invented! That, he said, he would never pay: not if his head was cut off and he was dragged naked through the streets of Tangier: not if the Sultan himself said he was to pay it. But the old Pilgrim became even more furious and insisted on being paid; and when the cobbler still refused, he called for the police and had him haled before the Pasha and sued him for the debt.

When the Pasha had listened to the case, he said: "This case is not one for me to judge, it is a case for Si Haman a-Filal!"

So both the litigants were seized by the police and taken to the house of Si Haman a-Filal. There Si Haman listened to them very carefully, and there was no doubt about it that both of them were in dead earnest. Then he gave judgment.

"There is no question," he said, "but that the Pilgrim is in the right. You, cobbler, must repay to the Pilgrim the debt which you owe him for the three days that he fed your canary. But," he said, turning on the triumphant Pilgrim, "there is a counter-claim. For three days this cobbler was without the song of his bird: that *you* must repay to *him*. I condemn you, therefore, to sit in a cage in the cobbler's shop, and sing to him for three days as well as his bird sings."

He then called the policemen over to him as if he had something of importance to say to them, leaving the Pilgrim unguarded; and when they looked round, needless to say, the Pilgrim was gone; nor did he ever trouble anyone in Tangier again.

The Story of Judah ben Hassan

THERE was once a man in Palestine who was married and had three sons. He died, and left much money. On his death they divided it among them. Two of them wasted their money in gambling; and when it was gone they came to the house of their mother and youngest brother and robbed them, and left them bare. So now Judah ben Hassan had nothing either, the unlucky man.

So he made a net to go fishing in a lagoon of the sea. In the same quarter of the town where he lived, there was a man who sold bread: and the days that Judah had caught fish he went there and bought a loaf: but the days that he caught nothing he went without.

One day the baker said to him, "Why is it that some days you buy bread, other days you don't?"

Judah answered, "The days that I catch fish, I have money to pay you. The days that I catch none I have none. That is why some days I buy bread, other days I don't."

So the baker said, "No, come for bread every day. The days you have money, pay me: when you have none, I will give you credit."

So Judah said, "Thank you," and came to an understanding with the baker.

One day that he was fishing in the lagoon there came to him a man, a Moor, riding upon a mule, with a rope of silk in his hands.

The man said, "Good day."

"Good day," said Judah ben Hassan.

"Are you Judah ben Hassan?"

He told him that he was.

Then the man said, "Take this rope, and tie my hands with it, and throw me in the sea. If I raise my hands, pull

on the rope and come in quickly and save me. But if it is
my feet you see above the water, then I am dead: take this
gold coin for your pains, and let the mule depart by itself."

Accordingly Judah flung him in the sea: and presently
saw his feet above the water. He was dead.

So Judah took the money, and let the mule depart by
itself, and went with the money to the house of the baker,
and paid what he owed.

Then he went to his mother, and told her what had
happened: "Today I was fishing, and there came a Moor
mounted on a mule, with a silk rope in his hands, and told
me to fling him in the sea. So when he was dead I took the
money he gave me, and let the mule depart alone."

But his mother said, "My son, beware of all Moors: for
I think he was up to some mischief."

"No, mother," said Judah. "I wish ten such Moors
would come to me every day: I would do to them as I did
to this one."

The next day he went again fishing in the lagoon, and
there came a second man, riding upon the same mule.
Everything happened as it did the day before: and when
Judah saw his feet he knew that he too was dead, and took
the money.

The third day there came a third man, and addressed
him as the other two. "Take this cord," he said, "and tie
my hands . . ."

"Yes," said Judah, "and throw you in the sea, like the
other two. There is no need to go through all that, I know
well by now what I have to do."

But the man continued, "Nevertheless, I must tell you
. . . If I raise my hands, come in quickly and save me: but
if I raise my feet, then you will know I am dead."

So Judah threw him in like the others: but instead of
his feet coming above the water, Judah saw his two hands:
and in them he was grasping a fish. So Judah went into the
lagoon and pulled him out.

Then the man said to him, "Come with me now to Fez.

With this fish that I have caught, we shall both be rich, and you will never need to go fishing again."

"No," said Judah, "I cannot go with you: for I have a mother, and she is poor, and will have nothing to eat, and my two brothers who are spendthrifts will rob her."

But the man said, "I will give you enough money for your mother until your return."

"Very well," said Judah, "I will tell all this to my mother. If she says I can go, I will go: if not, I will stay."

So he took the money that the man gave him to his mother, and told her everything.

"No, my son," said his mother, "don't go: for I am afraid that some evil will befall you there in Morocco."

"Let me go," said Judah: "for the man told me that if I went I should become rich: while now, some days I catch fish and others I catch none: but never again shall I catch such another chance as this."

"Very well," said his mother, "you can go."

So he told the man, "Yes: my mother will let me go with you."

Thereupon the two of them mounted together upon the mule, and they took with them no provision for the journey.

Presently Judah said, "I am hungry."

Then the man said to Judah, "Tell me: what would you like to eat?"

Then Judah answered, "I see nothing here to eat: if there were but a crust of bread, that were enough. Why do you ask me, 'What would you like to eat?' as if you were the host and a feast were spread?"

"All the same," said the man, "tell me what you would like to eat."

"I would like," said Judah, "first, chicken cooked with raisins. And then I would like mutton stewed with almonds and spices. And then I would like a little roast lamb."

So the man took his saddle-bags that were on the mule, and muttered something over them. Then he took out of them the very dishes that Judah had said he would most like. The two of them ate their fill: yet many fragments remained.

Then the man said, "Mount on the mule."

But Judah said, "And all the food that we have left uneaten?"

"Leave it," said the man. "If you are still hungry, eat more and welcome: but what you do not want to eat, leave it here on the ground."

So, the same day that they set out, they arrived at Fez. They went to the house of the man, and spent the night there.

In the morning the man said, "Do you know what we are going to do with this fish?"

"What?" said Judah.

"We are going to take it to the river, the Sebou, and cut it in the river, and burn incense on a brazier. Then the water will dry up: and when it dries up we shall see a door. You must go into that door alone: for it is written that no one may enter it but Judah ben Hassan only; and that was why I came to seek you: and I will remain here. At the door you will find a Negro slave, with a scimitar raised in his right hand. Have no fear of him: pass, and when you pass he will disappear. Then you will come to a second door: and there will be a Negress, who will look at you fiercely. Have no fear of her either: pass, and she too will disappear. Then you will come to a third door: and at this door you will find a woman wearing the appearance of your mother. Then she will weep and bewail and say, 'Alas! My son, why did you go away and leave me? I sorrowed for you, and so I came to seek you.' Then you will think that she is truly your mother: but take a sword that you will find there, and cry out, 'Strip off your clothes!' Then she will strip them off till she has only her chemise, at the same time weeping and reproaching you. Then threaten her with the sword and make her take off even her chemise: then she also will disappear. Then in the room beyond you will find gold, and silver, and jewels: and also a small box. Take for yourself whatever you will: bring me only that box."

So they went to the shores of the Sebou, taking with them a brazier. Then the man burnt incense on the brazier, and cut the fish in the river, and muttered to himself. Then the water of the river divided, and revealed a door, and the door opened.

So Judah entered the first door, and found the Negro, and passed to the second, and found the Negress, and arrived at the third. There he found the woman that appeared to be his mother. So he seized the sword and said, "Take off your dress!" Then the woman said, "My son, is that how you speak to your mother?" But he only replied, "Strip it off." So she began to undress, until she had nothing but a chemise. Then he said, "Take off that also." "Is that the way a son should treat a mother?" But he only answered, "Strip!" So she took off that also: and there was nothing there.

Then he found the box, and the gold and the silver and the jewels: but he left everything, and only took the box. Then he went back out of the cave, and gave the box to the man. In the box there were two rings.

Then the man said to Judah, "What will you take for your reward? Do you wish for gold and silver?"

"No," said Judah: "all I ask is the saddle-bags from your mule, and that you tell me how to use them."

So the man gave Judah the saddle-bags: and Judah said, "Now I wish to go to my home."

So the man gave him the mule, and said, "When you come to the gates of your town, let the mule go, to depart alone."

So Judah returned to his home, and at the gates of the town he let the mule go. He entered his house, and he found his mother, and told her all that had happened. Then he asked his mother if there was anything in the house to eat: but she said, "No."

So he took the saddle-bags, and muttered over them

what the man had taught him, and drew out every kind of victuals. Then his mother asked him, "Whence do these victuals come?" So he explained the whole thing to his mother, so that if she should be hungry at a time when he was not at hand, she also might get food out of the bags.

Then the other two brothers, who often had nothing to eat in their own houses, would come to their mother's; and there they would find the table spread with every kind of delicacy. Then they asked their mother, "Where does our brother get all these comforts?" And their mother told them the story of the saddle-bags. Then the two brothers plotted together, how they might get the saddle-bags for themselves: and one said, "I have a plan."

So he went down to the sea, and spoke to one of his acquaintance who was master of a ship. "I have a brother," he said, "who is a wastrel and a spendthrift and robs our mother: and if he be not somehow conveyed away from where he can harm us, we soon shall have nothing. Come, dine with us tonight: you will see how lavishly he spends all our substance on his stomach. After dinner, therefore, seize him, and carry him away on the ship with you."

Then the ship-captain agreed to the plan, and at nightfall he went to the house with his friend, and saw that what he said was true, that the table was spread with every kind of rarity and delicacy such as are only found on the tables of the very rich.

So between two and three o'clock of the morning they drugged Judah, and tied him with ropes, and carried him off to the ship.

In the morning Judah woke, and looked about him, and said, "Where am I?"

Then the Master of the ship reviled him, and said, "Thief!"

"How am I a thief?" asked Judah.

"Because you have spent your own patrimony, and now you steal the money of your brothers and your mother, and gamble it away, and spend it on rich foods when the very house over your head is tumbling down."

Then all Judah said was, "Misfortune comes from God": and he stayed with the ship, until a day came when the ship sank, and they were all drowned, except Judah who was washed up on the shore. Then he went into the town: till he found one who asked him, "Are you a native of this country?"

"No," said Judah, and told him all that had happened. So the man said, "If you like, you can come and work with me."

So Judah went with him.

But when Judah was carried off and put upon the ship, the next morning his brothers tried to take away the saddle-bags. At that the old woman cried out and tried to prevent them. Now the next house to theirs was the house of the Vizier: and when he heard the uproar he came out to enquire what was the matter: so the woman told him how the two men had shanghaied their brother, and now were trying to steal the saddle-bags. So the Vizier took the two brothers and put them in prison, and told the king the story. Then the Sultan said, "Take everything that there is in the house."

So the Vizier took it, and put it in the Sultan's treasury: and Judah's mother was left with nothing, so that every day she had to go and sit in the market-place with her hand out, crying to the passers-by to give her a piece of bread.

Meanwhile, Judah continued to work for the stranger in the strange city, until the time of the annual feast, when all the Mussulmen of the town go together to the cemetery: and there he found the first stranger, the man of Fez who had given him the saddle-bags.

"Peace be on you," said the man. "Is all well with you?"

"Peace be on you," said Judah. "Homage to God." Then he told the man all that had happened to him. Now the man was wearing on his finger the two rings that had been in the box that was behind the third door in the cave at the bottom of the Sebou: and he took off one of them and put it on the finger of Judah.

"Turn the stone towards the palm of your hand," said the man. This Judah did: and at once the earth opened, and there stood before him an enormous Djinn.

"What do you wish?" asked the Djinn.

"I should like to be at home in my own city," said Judah: and straightway found himself there, in the market-place where his mother sat begging for bread. There he found her, and she told him all that had happened: how his brothers had tried to carry off the saddle-bags, and how she cried out, and how the Vizier had come and haled them off to prison, and how the Sultan had sent and taken everything that there was in the house. Together they went back to their house: but it was empty, and in ill repair, and almost falling down.

Then Judah turned inwards again the stone of his ring, and summoned the Djinn, and ordered him to build a new house: a better house, he said, than any other in the town, even the Sultan's.

"It shall be ready by tomorrow morning," said the Djinn.

"Secondly," said Judah, "you are to go to the Sultan's treasury and bring to my house everything that you find within, both my own and of the Sultan's: and you are to go to the prison and bring my two brothers to me also."

All this the Djinn performed: before cock-crow the house was finished: then he went to the Sultan's treasury, and left it bare. Then he went to the prison: and there were the two brothers: and they felt a hand that they could not see take them each by the throat and convey them away through the air.

In the morning, the Sultan awoke, and the guardian of his treasure came to tell him the news.

"Who can it be," said the Sultan, "that can have entered into my treasure and done this to me?"

Then his Vizier answered him: "There is only one man that it can be. Last night my neighbour had a tumbledown hovel not fit for a dog, and today he has the finest palace in the city, finer even than yours."

"Who is this neighbour?" asked the Sultan.

"He is the brother of the two men you threw into prison," said the Vizier.

"Fetch them to me," said the Sultan. So they went to the prison to fetch them: but the chief warder told them, "In the night they are gone."

"So you see," said the Vizier, "it must be he."

Then the Sultan sent for the second Vizier, and said, "Take fifty men, and go to his house, and see if all this be true, and bring him to me."

So the second Vizier took fifty soldiers and went to the house of Judah ben Hassan. Before the door a small boy was lying upon the ground. He was so thin that you would have thought a breath would blow him away. Taking no notice of the child, the Vizier made as if to enter the house.

"What do you want?" asked the boy.

But the Vizier did not condescend to answer him.

So the boy stood up, and took the Vizier in his hands and flung him fifty feet back along the road he had come. Then he took a stick and beat the fifty soldiers with it, and they all ran away. The second Vizier returned to the palace of the Sultan, and told him what had happened.

"Take a hundred men, and go back again," said the Sultan. But the first Vizier stopped him. "No," he said. "If you send a thousand men, it will be the same. Judah ben Hassan is now a richer and more powerful man than you: he is more Sultan than you are."

"Then," said the Sultan, "let us devise some means by which he may take poison and die, and his wealth come to me."

"No," said the first Vizier: "but I will devise some other means by which all may turn out well for you."

So the first Vizier started out for the house of Judah ben Hassan: but instead of taking soldiers with him he went quite alone. He found the thin little lad lolling in front of the open door.

"Good day," said the Vizier. "Peace be on you."

"Peace be on you also," said the boy politely: "what do you seek?"

"I should like to speak with your master."

So then the boy rose up, and went in and told Judah what had happened. "First," he said, "there came a man with a rabble of fifty other men behind him, and tried to come in. So I beat them with a stick, and they ran away. Now there comes another man alone, and asks to speak with you."

"Let him come in," said Judah.

When the Vizier had come in to Judah, they exchanged greetings: and the Vizier saw all the gold and silver from the Sultan's treasury there in the house of Judah. Then he asked Judah why he treated the Sultan after this fashion.

"Why did the Sultan take everything that there was in my house, and leave my mother to beg for bread in the market-place?" asked Judah.

"With all respect," said the Vizier, "His Majesty did not take these things for himself. Your brothers were trying to take away everything and sell it: therefore the king put all your property into his treasury, to keep it safe till your return."

So Judah sent back the gold and silver of the king: and the Vizier went back and told the Sultan what had happened.

"Nevertheless," said the Sultan, "it were better to poison him: for if the people get to know this, that there lives in this city a man more rich and powerful than I am, then they will make him Sultan in my stead."

"No, Sidi," replied the Vizier, "that would not be right. But leave it to me: I will see to it that his power and his wealth come into your hands."

Then the Vizier went back to Judah, and told him that he came from the Sultan, and that the Sultan wished to come and take tea with him the next day.

"He is welcome," said Judah: and the next day the Sultan and all his court came and took tea with Judah.

Presently the Vizier came to Judah again and said, 'The Sultan has sent me to invite you to dine with him to-morrow."

Then the Vizier went to the Sultan, and spoke to him as follows: "Take your daughter, and dress her in gold and silks, and at the moment that Judah enters your house, let her run out from a chamber as if by accident."

The Sultan did as his Vizier advised him: and when Judah entered the palace in company with the Vizier, she ran out from a chamber as if she had not known they were there.

"What has happened?" said the Vizier to Judah.

"What has happened?" repeated Judah in surprise.

"Yes, for I saw your face change colour." Then the Vizier pretended for the first time to see the young princess. "Ah," he said, "it is the Sultan's daughter. So you would like to marry her? We will speak to the Sultan this very evening."

"Very well," said Judah.

So it was arranged that Judah should marry the Sultan's daughter: and for some time they all lived together in peace and happiness. But at last the old Sultan died. Then the Viziers and the people wished to make Judah Sultan: but he refused.

"I am rich," he said, "I am more powerful than any Sultan, and I am happy. Why should I trouble myself with the affairs of a kingdom?"

But they all importuned him; and at last he consented. The first thing he did was to raise his two brothers to the rank of Viziers.

But even so they were not content. "Why is it," said the eldest brother to the second, "that our brother is always one step above us? Now we are Viziers: but he is Sultan. Let us kill him, and then we can rule in his place."

So they invited him to dine at their house: and in the small hours of the morning they drugged him, and the eldest brother took the ring from his finger. Quickly he slipped it on his own, and summoned the Djinn.

"Take these men, both of them," he said, "and fling them into the middle of the Sahara."

So the Djinn flew away with Judah and the second brother also: but in the morning the first brother went up into Judah's house, and sat on Judah's throne: and when the Viziers and the people assembled he said, "Now I am the Sultan. And if you do not wish it, behold the ring." He raised his hand so that all could see the ring that was on his finger now.

So the people consulted together and said, "It were better to suffer him to be king than to face what evil he might do us with the ring."

Now the first act of Judah's brother, now that he was Sultan, was to wish to marry his brother's wife: which is not lawful until after three months have passed. The Cadis were at a loss what they should do: but the Sultan sent a message to them saying: "Give your consent: when the time comes, I shall know what to do."

So the Cadis gave their consent: and after the wedding they ate and drank together, and conversed until it was time to go to bed. Then the brother went to take hold of the Sultana: but she cried out and said, "Look! There he is!"

"Where? Who?" asked the brother.

"Your brother my husband," said the Sultana, "there, by the bed. Cannot you see him?"

"I see nothing," said the new Sultan. But every time he tried to touch her, she cried out that she could see her former husband standing there: and so an hour went by. At last she appeared to notice for the first time the ring on his finger.

"Ah," she said, "now I know why the ghost of my husband will not let us rest. Take off that ring, and he will disappear."

So the new Sultan, having grown very impatient by this time, took off the ring and the Sultana seized it and straightway summoned the Djinn.

"Where is my husband?" she asked.

"He is in the heart of the Sahara," replied the Djinn.

"Fetch him," said the Sultana: "and take this man and throw him as far away as possible: somewhere where not even you yourself could find him again."

So the Djinn despatched the wicked brother, and fetched back Judah. He was full of delight and gratitude, and held out his hand for the ring.

"No," said the Sultana: "anything you wish for you shall have: but the ring, that stays with me!"

. . . And Sidi Heyar had a Long Beard but Little Wits

THERE was once a Vizier called Sidi Heyar: and he had a long beard of which he was very proud. But one night as he lay awake reading in an old book, a history of times past, he came on the following sentence: 'And Sidi Heyar, the king's Vizier, had a long beard but little wits.' Now when Sidi Heyar saw this he was troubled. The name of this unfortunate Vizier of olden times was the same, and he, too, had a long beard: but there the likeness ended, for was it not on account of his prodigious wisdom that the king had made him Vizier? Nevertheless, supposing the king himself, through some whim, should read this very book, and come on this wretched sentence? He would be bound to take it for an omen, and draw from it conclusions to the detriment of his own, the wise Sidi Heyar.

In short, something must be done about it: but what? At first he thought of changing his name. But that would never do: he was too famous a man: everyone would continue to call him Sidi Hayer just the same.

The only thing, therefore, was to dispense with his long beard.

No sooner had Sidi Heyar taken this resolution than he reached out of bed and took up the candle that was burning beside it, at the same time passing his hand up and down his beard to decide how much of it he must sacrifice in order that it should no longer be possible to call it 'long'. When he had come to a decision he set light to the end of it, meaning to singe it that far and no further: but the flames took hold, and in a twinkling he had no more beard left than has a new-born baby. This was a great misfortune; for he could not leave the house until it had at least begun to grow again.

Moreover, when two days went by and he did not appear at the palace, the king began to enquire about him: and when the third day came and still no Sidi Heyar, the king and the court went in person to his house to ask what was the matter with him.

So Sidi Heyar muffled the lower part of his face in a handkerchief, and went out to receive the king.

"What is this?" said the Sultan: "why do you not come to my council?"

"Alas, Mulay," said Sidi Heyar, "I am very sick, and cannot leave my house."

"Then I will send the doctors to you," said the king: "and what is your sickness?"

"No, no," said Sidi Heyar: "it is no use sending a doctor to me: he cannot help me."

"Then what is this sickness of yours, that you are so anxious not to see a doctor?" asked the king.

At first Sidi Heyar was loath to tell him: but when the king threatened to cut off his head if he maintained silence, and to do the same if he said one word that was not the truth, at last he told him the whole story.

Then the king said, "Verily the ancient book was right. A man who burns off his beard with his bedside candle for such a reason is certainly not fit to be a Vizier of mine."

Then Sidi Heyar wept and besought him to give him another chance: and at last the Sultan said: "When you find another man called Sidi Heyar, who also has a long beard, and can beguile him into doing something even more foolish than you have done, then you can return into my favour."

So Sidi Heyar set out to find someone with the same name as himself, and a beard as long as his own had been. For a year he wandered about the city and country-side: but though he found many men with long beards, none of them was called Sidi Heyar: and at length when he found another Sidi Heyar, he was a young man with almost no beard at all.

But one day he was in the shop of a cloth merchant in a distant quarter of the city when he heard someone behind him say: "Show me that roll of red cloth, Sidi Heyar." "Take it, Sidi Mohammed," answered the merchant. "Feel what a fine weave it is."

Then Sidi Hayar looked: and behold, the merchant had a long grey beard that covered his chest and reached almost to his girdle. So he waited for a convenient moment, and then said to the merchant, "I am a stranger in this town": and claimed from him the hospitality which the Law enjoins on all Believers.

"You are welcome," said the merchant: and took him to his house with him. After he had eaten they drank tea together, and while they drank tea they conversed together. The Vizier told the merchant that he was a scribe; and moreover, a diviner.

"If you tell me your name," he said, "and the name of your mother, then I will read the future for you."

"My name is Heyar, the son of Zorah," said the merchant.

So the Vizier wrote on his tablets, and studied them, and wrote again. And then he said: "Within the next three days, you will receive unexpectedly both honey and silk."

Then they conversed of other things, and when night came they slept: but in the morning the Vizier went secretly to his own house and instructed his servants what they should do. He prepared a rich present of honey from the mountains and silks from France. "Take this," he said, "to such-and-such a house. And when they have opened the door, if they ask whence it comes, say it is the gift of God to Sidi Heyar."

So his servants did this; and when the servants of the merchant came and told him what had happened he was greatly surprised, for he recognised at once that the prophecy had come true: and he went in and told his wife. Then his wife said: "Ask the scribe to read his tablets again, and tell us something else that will happen."

So the Vizier studied his tablets again, and said, "Within three days you will have sold everything you have in your shop, and at whatever prices you ask."

Again he instructed his servants: and this time they went to the merchant's cloth-shop, not together but separately, and each bought something, till at last the shop was bare—nothing left in it at all except the merchant himself. There the Vizier found him: and asked him why his shop was empty. Then the merchant, in great wonder, told him that his second prophecy also had come true.

That evening, the merchant asked the Vizier to read his tablets a third time, and Sidi Heyar did so. But instead of announcing something to the merchant as before, he tore up the tablets and flung them away, an expression of great sadness on his face. Then the merchant was very anxious to know what he had read: and at last the Vizier took fresh tablets, and wrote on them, and read them again. But again he tore them into small pieces and flung them away with a look of the utmost melancholy. But when the merchant would not cease importuning him he at last consented to read them a third time, and tell the merchant what he saw.

"On the third day from now, Sidi," he said, "between two and three in the morning, you will die. But because your life has been a good and a holy one, God will do with you what He only does with saints: though dead, you will continue conscious of the world around you, able to hear everything said about you both good and evil: only you will not be able to reply."

When the merchant heard this he was very sad, and went in and told his wife that in three days he would be dead. Then his wife said, "Perhaps it is not true." But the merchant pointed out to her that the other two prophecies had both come true: so why would not this one? Then he remained in his chamber for the three days that followed, preparing himself for death: and allowed no one to come in to him except the Vizier only.

On the third day, at two in the morning, the Vizier laid

down the Koran which he had been reading aloud to the unhappy man, and prepared a drink of hashish, and gave it to him, "in order," he said, "that the pains of Death may not be too severe."

Then he took a needle, and thrust it into the merchant's big toe.

The merchant cried out, and asked, "What is that?"

"That is the first pang of Death," said the Vizier: "He is entering by your big toe."

Then he took the needle and drove it into his knee, and told him that Death had now reached that far. Presently he pricked him in the stomach. "Death," he said, "has now reached your body." At last he pricked him in the neck. "Now," he said, "it is all over: you are dead."

So he sent a message to the merchant's wife that she was now a widow; and they fetched water from the baths, and he bathed the body of the merchant, and tied his toes together, and wound him in a winding-sheet. "Remember," he said, "that though you know everything that is going on, and can hear everything that is said of you, both good and ill, it is no use attempting to reply."

Then he fixed the time of the funeral, and went out into the town.

The first thing he did was to collect about thirty beggars, and promise them a dollar apiece if they did as he told them. "When you see a funeral coming, ask who is dead; and when they tell you it is Sidi Heyar, ask which Sidi Heyar; and when they tell you it is the rich cloth merchant, who had his house in such-and-such a quarter, then begin all together to revile him as loudly as ever you can: leave no word of abuse that ever you have heard spoken, or that you can imagine, unsaid."

Then the Vizier sent a message to the Sultan, to be waiting at the gate of the city towards the cemetery at a certain hour, that he might see what would befall.

When the funeral procession, singing dirges and mourning dolefully, came to the gate, the crowd of beggars was waiting.

"Who are you burying?" they called to the bearers.

"We are burying Sidi Heyar," they answered.

"Which Sidi Heyar is that?"

"The rich cloth merchant, who dwelt in such-and-such a quarter."

Then the beggars began to revile him with one voice. "That son and grandson of whores? So he has got his deserts at last! Many is the time I have asked him for a crust of bread and he has answered, 'God will feed you,' and when I asked him again he struck me and thrust me under his mule! Rich? But where did his riches come from? Not from God! He grew rich by robbing the widow and the orphan, by swindling and cheating, by mixing hemp with his wool, by shortening his yardstick—"

For a time the corpse suffered all this in silence: but at last he could contain himself no longer. He sat up on the bier and cried out:

"It is you that are sons of whores, the whole pack of you, to tell such lies about me! If I were not dead, well I know how I would punish you for this! It is only because I am dead, and you know that I cannot hurt you, that you dare to say such things!"

Then the bearers, in surprise and terror, let him fall to the ground.

"What is the matter?" he asked them: "what did you drop me for? Come, pick me up and let us get on with this funeral: put me quickly somewhere where I cannot hear all these lies and wickednesses."

"But where do you want us to carry you?" asked the bearers.

"Why to the cemetery of course, where I belong."

"If you want to go there," said one of the bearers, "you must walk there: which you look to me well able to do."

Then they all broke and fled, leaving the merchant to walk home as best he could in his winding-sheet: and the Sultan laughed loudly and received the Vizier back into his favour.

The Cow

OF late years the Government has become a robber of men, but it was not always so. A hundred years ago there was a Pasha who ruled Tangier whose word was righteous and whose hand was mighty, so that all evildoers feared him.

There were living at that time in one of the villages of Anjera that came under his control two brothers who were robbers; and one night they were walking abroad when they came upon a cow.

"Brother," said the first, "let us steal this cow."

"No," said the second robber, "for I see the Pasha sitting beside it."

"What nonsense," said the first brother: "the Pasha is at home in his house in Tangier, asleep: how should he be sitting beside this old cow far from the town in the nighttime?"

"Nevertheless," said the second brother, "it is as I say; or at least if we steal that cow, it will be as bad for us as if the Pasha were indeed sitting by it to guard it."

But the first brother paid him no heed, and stole the cow, and hid it in a safe place in the mountains, and returned to his village. Now the cow belonged to an old woman of that same village who had neither husband nor son; and in the morning when she went out to milk it, behold, there was no cow! When she found it was gone she did not hesitate what to do. She tucked up her skirts for the journey and took a staff in her hand and started out for the city of Tangier.

Now the brother who had stolen the cow was watching her to see what she would do; and as she passed him he greeted her, and said:

"Where are you going, Beautiful One?"

"Allah knows where I am going," she replied: "and *I* know where I am going. That is two who know; and two is enough. Why should you know also?" And she went on her way. She crossed the mouth of the river, and she entered the city, and she climbed up the steep streets to the Palace of the Pasha, and was brought before him.

"What do you want?" he asked her.

"Give me back my cow!" she said roughly; "the cow you stole from me last night!"

"What?" said the Pasha, "the cow that *I* stole? What is this?"

"The cow that you stole," she repeated stubbornly. "*You* are the Pasha; the Government of this country is in your hands; whatever is stolen, therefore, is stolen by *you*."

At this the Pasha groaned, feeling that there was a kind of truth in her words, and stroked his beard and thought a while.

"Tell me," he said, "do you know who did this?"

"No," she replied, "I have no idea."

Then he thought a little longer.

"Did anyone speak to you this morning as you left your village?" he asked.

"Yes," she said, "one man spoke to me."

"And what did he say?"

"He asked me where I was going."

"Go!" said the Pasha to one of his soldiers, "and fetch me that man."

So the soldier went straight to the house of the robber and fetched him before the Pasha; and for all I know he is in prison still; for it is certain he was put into prison that very day, and I never heard that he was let out.

The Vizier's Razor

THERE was once a poor man who became, owing to the excellence of his work, barber to the Sultan at Fez. And he became a great favourite with the Sultan, who loved him and trusted him.

Now every day when the Sultan went abroad into the city, he passed a certain shop: and he was astonished each day to see that the shop was empty—there were no goods in it of any kind, yet the shopkeeper sat cross-legged upon the counter as if waiting for customers. So, one day, the Sultan called one of his soldiers, and asked him what this strange shopkeeper could be selling. The soldier did not know: so the Sultan sent him to enquire.

The soldier went up to the shopkeeper and addressed him imperiously: "Our Lord asks what you sell in your shop. Answer me truthfully, that I may tell our Lord; for *I* think that you sell nothing, and are no true shopkeeper but one who goes out at night robbing and cutting people's throats, and doing other wickedness!"

"Tell our Lord," replied the shopkeeper, in no way perturbed, "that I sell words."

So the soldier went back and told the Sultan what the shop-keeper had said.

"Ask him the price of his words," said the Sultan; and the soldier went back to the shopkeeper.

"I sell them," said the shopkeeper, "for a hundred pieces of gold per portion."

When the soldier told this to the Sultan, the Sultan called for his purse, and counted out a hundred pieces of gold, and told the soldier to buy him a portion. When the soldier gave the money to the shopkeeper he counted it carefully and put it in his satchel and said to the soldier:

"Tell to our Lord, '*Never act in haste: think first*'."

So the soldier returned to the Sultan and gave him the portion of words which he had bought. The Sultan was so pleased with his purchase that he had it inscribed everywhere in his Palace. It was written upon the floors and the walls in mosaic; it was carved upon the ceilings; it was woven in the curtains; it was painted on the dishes; it was embroidered upon the very towels.

Now the Sultan had a Vizier who was jealous of the barber's favoured position. "Even as a barber," said the Vizier to himself, "the Sultan favours him more than he does me. What is to prevent a day coming when the Sultan sends me packing, and makes the barber Vizier in my stead?" Such a thing seemed to the Vizier very regrettable, since he was himself a wise and politic statesman, loved and feared by the people of Fez even more than the Sultan himself—so that he had hopes that when the Sultan (who had no son) should die, they might make him Sultan himself.

So one day he called the barber as he was leaving the Sultan's Palace.

"I have often seen you coming and going from shaving His Majesty," he said, "but I have never had an opportunity of seeing the razor and the scissors you use. Surely you do not use the same ones for His Majesty as you use for common people?"

"No, certainly not," said the barber; "I keep a special razor and special scissors for the Sultan, the best that I have."

And he set down his case and opened it to show them to the Vizier. The Vizier picked up the razor and looked at it with a glowering countenance.

"Are you not ashamed to use upon the head of His Majesty such a very ordinary razor as this one?" he said.

"Alas," said the barber, "I am a poor man. It is a good razor, the best razor I have . . ."

Then the Vizier laid his hands on the barber's shoulders in a friendly fashion and said:

"Come, my friend, this will not do. I will myself give you a razor with a handle of gold and set with stones, a razor more worthy than this of shaving His Majesty's head."

The barber was overcome with gratitude; and even more so when after a few days the Vizier's gift arrived. He put it in his case the next time he went to shave the Sultan.

Now the method of his work was this. First he laid his tools upon a cushion where they should be ready to hand; then the Sultan's personal slaves tied the towel round the Sultan's neck, and the barber with his fingers worked the soap into the hair of the Sultan's head to soften it. As he was thus soaping the Sultan's head, the Sultan's eyes were caught by the magnificent new razor. But the barber's own eyes were caught by the words embroidered on the towel round the Sultan's neck: '*Never act in haste: think first*': and he began to murmur them to himself as his fingers were rubbing the Sultan's scalp.

'Never act in haste: think first.' Purposely the barber left the jewelled razor lying upon the cushion, and picked up the old one with which to shave the Sultan.

"Tell me," said the Sultan, "why do you do that? Why don't you use that fine new razor?"

"Wait a minute," said the barber, who was an artist and intent upon his work: "Wait till I have finished."

So in silence he completed the shaving of the Sultan.

"My only reason," he said, "was this. It is true I brought that new razor to use upon your head: but then I read the words embroidered upon the towel, and I thought: 'Why should I make any change? The old razor is a good one: I know it: the new one I don't know.'"

"How did you come by the new razor?" asked the Sultan.

The barber told him the whole story.

"I see," said the sultan, stroking his newly curled beard. Suddenly he clapped his hands, and a slave darted forward.

"Call the Vizier," said the Sultan.

"The slave ran to the Vizier's house and in a very short time the Vizier was before His Majesty.

"I think," said the Sultan, looking closely at the Vizier's face, "I think, my friend, you need a shave."

"Whatever you say is true, Lord," replied the Vizier; "but I was shaved this very morning."

"Never mind," said the Sultan, "I still think you need a shave; and my friend here will do it."

So the Vizier sat down before his master, and the slaves put a towel round his neck, and the barber soaped his head. When all was ready, the barber picked up his trusted old blade with which to shave the Vizier.

"No!" said the Sultan. "He thought that razor not worthy to shave *my* head, and himself gave you that fine new one, handled with gold and encrusted with diamonds. Now I too say that old blade is not worthy to shave the head of so faithful a subject! Take the new razor."

Thereupon, the barber shaved the Vizier as his master directed; and in doing so he made a small scratch on the Vizier's scalp. Hardly had it happened when the Vizier was seized with tremors and paroxysms, and shortly expired. The blade of that razor was poisoned.

Whereupon the Sultan made the barber Vizier in his place, and observed to his courtiers: "When I paid a hundred pieces of gold for those words, you thought them expensive. It seems to me now that I bought them cheaply enough!"

The Eyes of Ben 'Adi

THERE was once an Arab called Ben 'Adi; and he was amongst those who put very little trust in women. For a long time he said he would never marry at all—because, he said, if he had a wife he would never trust her: and what would be the use of that?

"If I do marry," he said, "it shall never be a grown woman, but some child who will grow up never to have seen any other man but myself."

The more he thought about this plan, the more it seemed to solve his difficulties; so at last he spoke to a friend of his who had a daughter who was nine years old, whose name was Zorah, and asked for her in marriage.

"But that is impossible!" replied his friend. "She is only a child, she is not yet of marriageable age."

Then Ben 'Adi explained his reasons and said:

"If I marry her, she shall live with me as my daughter until she is old enough to be my wife, never seeing any other man but myself; and so I think I may succeed in bringing up a wife for myself in whom I may trust."

To this the father agreed, and Ben 'Adi took his young wife home, and the years went by till she grew to womanhood: and all that time Ben 'Adi never allowed any other man to enter the house, not even his own brother: and when he went out he invariably locked the door and carried the key in his hand.

Now at the time Zorah came to womanhood there were four young bachelors who had taken the house next door to Ben 'Adi. Their life was a gay one, and it was their custom frequently to entertain women of the town and to play the lute and sing until sunrise. This was something of a nuisance to Ben 'Adi; but it was a wonderful thing to Zorah, who had never heard music or singing in her life

before, except for the lullabies sung to her in her cradle—
and the songs the four young bachelors sang were very
different to these. So presently she took a skewer and made
for herself a small hole in the wall between the houses. At
first she put her ear to it, to listen to the music; but
presently she put her eye to it to see what was going on.
Thus, when her husband was out, she often used to watch
the festivities unobserved. But the hole was small, and
presently she enlarged it to be able to see better; and at
last it was so big that the four young bachelors discovered
it. Thereupon they began to talk to her, and one of the
young bachelors fell very much in love with this eye which
he could see through the hole in the wall; and Zorah fell
in love with him.

The bachelors invited Zorah to come in and join their
junketing.

"How can I?" said Zorah: "every time my husband
goes out he locks the door and takes the key with him."

But presently she thought of a plan.

When her husband came home he found her very sulky,
and complaining very much of the lack of ornament in his
house.

"In my father's house," she said, "all the walls are hung
with tapestry; but here there is nothing but ugly white-
wash."

So Ben 'Adi, anxious to content her, bought a fine wall-
hanging; and this she stretched across the wall against the
bachelors' house. No sooner was this done than she set to
work from her side, and the bachelors from the other, and
soon they had made the hole large enough for her to pass
through; and on their side also they concealed it with a
wall-hanging. Thus, when Ben 'Adi was away by day at his
work, or at night visiting his friends, Zorah was able to slip
through into the next house; and a great deal of fun she
had there. And the young bachelors amused themselves
by composing mocking verses about Ben 'Adi.

At last one of them hit upon a plan to make even greater

mock of him, and proposed that they should invite Ben 'Adi to the house when his wife was actually there! So they trumped up an acquaintance with him, and began to invite him to visit them. At first he refused; but they would accept no refusal, and at last he came in to drink tea with them. The young men were too cunning to allow Zorah to be present on this occasion, or, indeed, on the first two or three times that Ben 'Adi visited them. They had other girls instead to sing with them and render the occasion festive.

But at last an evening came when Ben 'Adi said to Zorah that he was going next door to spend the evening with the young bachelors, who were not at all such bad fellows as he had at first supposed. Thereupon he went out and locked the door, and knocked at the door of the next house. This, of course, took him a minute or two; and while he was doing it Zorah slipped through the hole in the wall; and, when they admitted Ben 'Adi, she was sitting with the young men, and pouring out tea for them, as if she had been there a long time. When Ben 'Adi saw her he was thunderstruck at the resemblance to his wife, and muttering some excuse or other he dashed back to his own house. There he found Zorah patiently sewing; and was even more thunderstruck than before.

"What is the matter?" said Zorah. "Are you ill? Have you seen a ghost or a djinn, or some strange sight?"

"Indeed I have seen a strange sight!" said Ben 'Adi; "for I thought I saw *you* sitting in the house next door."

"Are you mad?" said Zorah. "How could that be, when you have locked me into this house?"

"There is a woman next door," said Ben 'Adi; "not only is her face exactly like yours, she is even dressed exactly as you are!"

"That is strange indeed," said Zorah: "your eyes must have deceived you."

"Indeed they did!" said Ben 'Adi. "But it is now plain to me that when Allah made you He must have made not one of you but two!"

"Perhaps," said Zorah, "when He made me, He forgot that He had done so, and immediately did it again."

Then Ben 'Adi returned to the bachelors' house.

"What was the matter?" they cried out: "why did you leave us so suddenly?"

Ben 'Adi muttered excuses even more foolish than those he had made before; and Zorah (who was of course again sitting there) handed him a cup of tea with her own hand.

"To the eyes of Ben 'Adi!" she said as she gave it him; and as if this was a toast, all four of the bachelors repeated it as they drank their tea.

Thus the evening passed very pleasantly for all of them; but at last Ben 'Adi said it was time for him to go home, as it was late, and his wife would be asleep, and if she woke in the night and found him not there, she would be afraid.

"I am sure," said Zorah, "that your wife is not asleep. What! a wife sleep when her husband is feasting in the very next house?—I feel certain," she said, "you will find her awake when you get back, and sitting up for you."

So Ben 'Adi waited a bit longer; and when he returned to his house he found Zorah still sitting there sewing.

"How does this seem," she said, holding up her work, "to the eyes of Ben 'Adi?"

"How is it, my love," said Ben 'Adi, "that you are still awake?"

"How could I sleep with all the noise and riot that is going on next door? I tell you, go to those young men and ask them to stop their singing, so that honest folk may get a little sleep at night."

"No," said Ben 'Adi; "they are young, and it is right that they should enjoy themselves." (For now that he was a partner in their enjoyment he no longer thought it so great a nuisance as he had at first.)

This went on for some time. Ben 'Adi and Zorah and the four young bachelors frequently sat up together until late in the night. But during this time the love between Zorah and the youngest of the bachelors increased; and at length

they decided to flee together into another city. Now these
four bachelors were like four brothers: where one went,
they all went. They therefore began to prepare to take
their departure; and they told Ben 'Adi, of course, what
they intended—excepting only that they told him it was
Rabat they were going to, when really their destination was
Meknes. At last the day came when they said to Ben 'Adi:

"Tomorrow at dawn we depart, and it may be that we
shall never see thee again, O Brother. Come, therefore, and
spend the whole night with us; and let us have a last feast
together, and let us depart from Tangier under the blessing
of the eyes of Ben 'Adi."

All this, of course, Ben 'Adi told his wife.

"I am very glad," she said, "that they are going. Once
they are well away from Tangier my heart will be much
lighter; but I am afraid that life will seem sad and dull to
you, my lord!"

Ben 'Adi, of course, thought that she meant that she
herself would sleep more soundly when there was no more
singing in the small hours, while he would find life dull
without their pleasant company. He did not read the
meaning in her words. So, feeling very fondly towards her,
he left her and went in to spend his last night with the four
bachelors. There, of course, he found Zorah helping the
bachelors to pack their belongings; and indeed she had
with her a bundle of her own, and told Ben 'Adi that she
was travelling with them.

"That, of course," said Ben 'Adi, "is as it should be."

But it seemed that the young men and Zorah herself
could do nothing without his help. Whether it was a
bundle to be corded, or a garment to be folded, or mules
to be hired, they kept asking his assistance. "Let everything," they said, "be done under the eyes of Ben 'Adi,
and so it shall be well done!"

But at last dawn came, and all was ready; and Ben 'Adi
kissed the four bachelors and wished them Godspeed, and
they set off; with Zorah on a mule with them, waving to him.

It was now time for Ben 'Adi to go to his work; so he did so at once without returning to his house, and did not get back there till the evening. When he did, of course, he found Zorah gone. He supposed that she must be visiting her own family; so he went to the house of his father-in-law, and knocked at the door, and asked whether Zorah was there.

"How should Zorah be here?" said her father: "never do you allow her to visit us! When you go out you lock her into the house as if she were a prisoner."

"That is true," said Ben 'Adi; "but I thought perhaps I had forgotten to lock the door; for she is certainly gone!"

Then his father-in-law came at him in a rage, and cried: "*Thou* askest *me* where is Zorah? It is *I* should ask *thee* what has thou done with our daughter! For years thou hast not let us see her: and now thou comest, and sayest: she is gone!" And the old man seized Ben 'Adi by the shoulders, and shook him in his anger.

Then Ben 'Adi returned to the streets and wandered about the whole town asking all he met if they had seen her. But how should any man in Tangier know if he had seen her or not? Since Ben 'Adi had always kept her locked in his house, there was not a man who had ever caught a glimpse of her.

Then Ben 'Adi, sad and weary, returned to his empty house and sat down there: and as he was sitting there came a wind which blew through from the house next door, and made the wall-hanging waver. Then Ben 'Adi tore it down, and saw the hole, and knew what had happened: and his grief was so great that he was like a man who is mad. All the time those words which had been used so often, 'the eyes of Ben 'Adi', kept ringing through his head: and going to the fire he took the skewer with which Zorah had first made the hole, and fanning the charcoal to a blaze he made it red hot; and then touched both his eyes with it, so that he was blind.

A Woman to Talk to

IT is a shocking thing to come by chance, in a melancholy
place, on the bones of an old acquaintace. It happened
to me on a journey I made last year; and the single inci-
dent sufficed to bring back to my mind this whole strange
story. I had thought it all finished eight years ago, violently
and finally—I never expected the curtain to go up again,
in this way, on a kind of epilogue.

Cutting off the secure and fertile plains of the French
Protectorate of Morocco from the rest of Africa stands the
enormous wall of the Atlas Mountains: snow-capped peaks
of crimson rock, towering fourteen thousand feet high. I
had reached the middle of one of the broad and desolate valleys that lie beyond this range, between it and
the lesser ranges of the Anti-Atlas that fringe the true
Sahara.

It was early in the morning; but the air still held, under
its heavy blanket of black cloud, the stale heat of yesterday.
There was no sun; but there was no hope of rain. For seven
years, now, no rain had fallen here. The dusky black sky
continually bore it away northward, to the mountains and
to the green plains beyond.

Yet once even this valley must have been fertile: for
here at my feet lay the walls of a vast, ruined palace. The
surface of the great dune of sand that now overtopped it
stirred a little, like the skin of an animal, under the irrita-
tion of the parched south wind.

There was nothing to be heard there but this wind, and
the harsh dry rattle of a flurry of locusts—lost stragglers
from the billions of the main swarm. As my feet trod
amongst them, they rose for a few moments into the air;
but they soon settled again. They were too weak, now, for
flight. Yet their idiot, armour-plated faces could give no

expression to the pangs of hunger which were killing even them in this desolate place.

Drifts of them lay in every hollow of the sand where the wind had left them. Brown patches of them stained the broken flat roofs of the palace.

Most of the Palace was buried in sand: and in the courtyard only the capitals showed above it of those slender marble columns which had once formed cool colonnades.

In one place, however, just inside the fallen gateway, some freak of the wind had newly eddied out of a deep pit, which reached right down to the glittering green mosaic pavement beneath. At the edge of this bare patch lay a roundish, white object. But it was not till I looked at it carefully that I saw what it was—a skull, scoured and polished by the sand that had buried it, and had now in such a strange way revealed it again. Some grim trophy, I supposed at first, fallen from the once-triumphal arch of the palace gate.

I did not expect, in that place of bones, to meet with any other life than what was left in those dying insects. Yet suddenly, from a sort of burrow in the sand leading to an inner chamber, a woman appeared, dressed in the blue rags of the Saharan tribes, her face, and even her eyes, covered in a fold of the blue canvas stuff against the devilish clouds of dust.

Then she too saw the skull.

The bones of men and even animals are not an uncommon sight in these deserts, but her whole attitude changed. She stiffened into a curious intentness, throwing back her veil and gazing at the object in a fixed way. No one could have doubted, who saw her like this, that she knew at once for certain whose bone this must be.

From the same hole in the sand a man appeared, as gaunt and sand-dried as herself. He called her twice, by name: "*Heba! Heba!*" But she did not move.

Prompted by that strange intentness of hers, it was then

I too realised, in a sudden flash, the whole past scene. The fear-maddened tribesmen at the gate—why, it was there *he* would have stood to meet them. The sudden volley. The pillage. And that strange shutting-up of the heavens, like a curse, which had so quickly turned this once lovely garden and all this fertile province into desert. I seemed to see the captive sand, seven years ago, freeing itself little by little from the withered roots that held it, beginning to grow active. First, clouds of dust—little whorls that moved a few yards among the shrivelled trees and died. Then, as it broke through all restraint, sand-waves accumulating forty feet high, slowly animated by the wind, advancing inch by inch; filling the dry river-bed, piling up against the palace wall, breaking its roofs by their weight, burying the painting, burying carved pillars, mosaic floors, honeycomb ceilings of cedar-wood.

Almond trees and olives; argan, cedar and palms; fields of barley and millet irrigated by little trickling rills from the river: after a few years of drought the only thing left of those cool and stately groves would be a few whitened spars all awry.

A little of this history I had seen myself. Part I gathered from hearsay. The rest I learnt then and there, when I camped for a day and a night with Abdselam and Heba in those forlorn and rubbishy ruins.

ii

Many years ago, before the French occupation, the old Kaid of Medoula, Omar's father—a well-meaning and impoverished puppet, ground between the nether stone of his own unruly tribesmen and the upper one of the Sultan's government—was travelling north to placate the latter. My uncle, Sir Robert Penn, was travelling south, through the unknown Atlas Mountains, to placate his own spirit.

Emerging suddenly from a narrow defile, Uncle Robert came on a strange scene.

On a ledge of rock stood, stock still, a valuable black slave. His face was that peculiar, smoky-grey colour that a Negro's face goes when he is thoroughly frightened. Carefully balanced between his ankle-bones he held a smallish egg.

Fifty yards off a wild young scaramouche in a ragged jelaba levelled an antiquated, silver-mounted flint-lock. *Bang!* The egg was shattered: the Negro unscratched.

The sport of the thing, of course, was this—that a valuable black slave with a splintered ankle-bone is a valuable slave no longer; and the wrath of an Arab father is not a light thing to risk. My uncle took a liking to the lad on the spot.

It was the beginning of one of those very rare friendships which sometimes do link men of different race. There grew up a singular confidence between them. Indeed, I doubt whether either of those two in his whole life ever had a closer friend than the other.

They were alike in personal bravery, and in that general quality of force and strength which makes a man stand out from his fellows. But in every other way they were utterly unlike. My uncle, for instance, made it his gentle boast that he had never, in a long life of adventure and exploration, killed a man, even in self-defence. Omar el Medouli (who never boasted) did not only kill men for reasons of state—he sometimes killed them for whim. My uncle, whose position at the Moorish Court gave him every opportunity of enriching himself, never took a penny from friend or enemy: the thumbscrew and the dagger were reputable among the instruments which Omar—that obscure younger son of a Southern chieftain—used to build his colossal fortune. My uncle, who never married, treated all women with a kind of frightened—almost rude —friendliness. A whole staff of secretaries were occupied in the recruiting of Omar's harem.

Furthermore, my uncle had no belief whatever in the

existence of God: while Omar's belief in God was the first
root of his being.

When someone at last killed that obscure old man his
father with an axe, Omar found, among his many brothers,
only two formidable rivals to the succession. By the will of
God the elder of these two, when tied up and made to
watch how the younger died, went mad—he is alive
today in an asylum near Ascot. This caused many tribesmen who had paid scant allegiance to the father to
recognise in Omar a leader they could really hate and
respect.

Soon, in the wild South-west beyond the mountains, the
Sultan's writ ran only by his good pleasure; and that good
pleasure was not cheaply come by. In short, he rapidly
established for himself in the Anti-Atlas and the Sous the
same kind of position that Raisuli had in the North: but
with a more powerful intellect than Raisuli's, and longer
policies, it was obvious that he was capable of going much
further.

By the time I first came to Morocco myself (visiting my
uncle one school holidays) the name of Omar el Medouli
was already one of the first four or five in the country, and
Omar's friendship with my uncle one of many years'
standing.

It was a friendship necessarily of a peculiar character.
As Omar increased in temporal greatness, the two often
found themselves political opponents. Even then they
never did each other direct harm, nor told each other lies
—nor, by the same token, did either ever ask the other a
question which could serve his own advantage: their
friendship was built as much on the capacity of both for
silence and reserve as on anything else.

My uncle once told me a story which illustrates this
strange reticence. He was staying at a little castle the Kaid
owned near Mogador, recovering from the bullet a
fanatical Soussi had put in his leg. Presently orders arrived
from the Kaid at Medoula that the Governor of the castle

(an old man, and the Kaid's own cousin) was to be beaten
to death—gradually, morning and evening.

Dawn found my uncle breakfasting in the wretch's cell.
The executioners arrived. My uncle forbade them to touch
the prisoner. By whose authority? By none—except his
own.

The executioners were nonplussed: "If we disobey the
Kaid, he will kill us." "That is not my affair; I don't care
whether he kills you or not. I only say that you are not to
touch this man."

This was a bold action for a man in a country where the
name of a Christian was the name of a dog, and where his
own safety depended on the authority of the very Kaid he
was flouting.

Presently the executioners lost heart: the prisoner was
released.

But the odd thing about the whole story is this: when the
Kaid himself arrived a few weeks later, the subject was
never mentioned between them, neither by the one nor the
other. The old man, received back into favour as if
nothing had happened, never thanked my uncle nor
showed any other sign of gratitude; and my uncle never
learned on what charge he had, perhaps most deservedly,
been condemned.

My anxiety to meet the Great Kaid was by no means
decreased by the stories I heard of his cruelties. To the
bloodthirsty mind of an English schoolboy they even gave
him a kind of sultry halo. So, when I was told one day that
he would lunch with all of us the next, my excitement was
intense. For it is not every little British schoolboy, I felt,
who is privileged to sit cross-legged on a cushion, and dip
his hand in the dish with a man who has tortured his
fellow-men to death: a man reputed—oh ironic boast!—
the finest spearman of this our twentieth century.

I was standing close to my uncle as he greeted his guest.
Kaid Omar el Medouli, Prince of the Anti-Atlas and
Pasha of Taroudant, was a majestic figure in his beautifully

cut robes of black and the purest white, a curved
dagger in a plain silver sheath hung round his neck on a
dark silk cord. So much I knew already from pictures; but
I was not prepared for that long, thin, dark face under the
white hood; the gentle and inexpressibly melancholy eyes;
the mouth, that in moments of relaxation hung crookedly
(a nerve in his face had been severed in some fight, so that
only a superhuman effort could hold it straight).

But it was not till we were moving from the gate, slowly
and with many pauses, followed at a little distance by the
silent knot of Medouli's councillors, to the room where we
should lunch, that I caught sight for the first time of his
left hand, half hidden in his wide sleeve. Shrivelled and
scarred, it looked as if it had been thrust, long ago, into a
furnace.

That hand fascinated me. What desperate occasion had
so maimed it? What heroic deed?

I knew no Arabic: and the conversation was in Arabic.
But already, with a child's acuteness of ear, I could distinguish the harsh burr of my uncle's accent—that of a
northern Moor, a Riffian—from the quiet, water-like
tones of the Southerner. They spoke little while eating—
Arab manners forbid: conversation waits for the glasses of
sweet tea that follow, and my thoughts never left that
hand.

With the tea, Medouli spoke to me, in English: and I,
with a rudeness unthinkable in one of his own race,
burst out immediately about his hand—how had it happened?

In a gentle, apologetic voice he told me that when a lad,
no bigger than myself, he had been reaching to toast a
skewer of meat over a hot stove, and had fallen forward,
his hand right in the heart of the glowing charcoal.

Disappointed, ashamed, and confused with a belated
shyness, I said no more. How I hated my uncle's sarcastic
old face, grinning at me when he caught my eye!

For a moment, just before our guest left, I was left alone

with him. On a table lay a beautifully illuminated old Koran, that my uncle had somehow contrived to buy. Omar el Medouli, without speaking to me, picked it up, kissed it reverently, put it in his sleeve, and walked out of the house: and further I *knew* he meant me to see what he did.

When my uncle returned, however, and before I could tell him of the startling thing I had witnessed, he took me none too gently by the shoulder, and told me just how rude my curiosity had been. Then, the scolding over, he began patting my arm. Then swung me round to face him, and said in a very different tone:

"Now shall I tell you the truth about that hand?"

I was surprised. "What! was that not the truth, then?" It hardly seemed to me the kind of story a man would make up.

"The truth," said my uncle, "is this. Once, when Omar was a young man, he was besieged in a small fortress in the mountains. It was about to be taken by storm. He sent his men out quietly, during the night, waited behind alone, and blew the place up as the enemy entered."

"Then why . . .?"

"No, it wasn't to chide your manners. It is simply that his hatred of boasting amounts almost to a mania. You would never guess, from his talk, that he had smelt powder in his life."

My uncle paused.

"Contrary to all Moslem practice, he once let me see him stripped. You could not have laid the spread palm of your hand on an area of skin that had not its scar."

Not till then was I able to tell my uncle about the strange theft I had witnessed. He swore testily.

"What a fool I was to leave it about!" he said. "But Omar was right. It would have been an impious act for him to leave it in the hands of an Unbeliever." He paused, and made a wry face. "It cost me a hundred and fifty pounds," he added.

Then, as we parted: "I wish I had a God I could serve as Omar serves his!"

What did he mean? My uncle had a way of making remarks like this with such a diabolically ironical expression I never dared ask him to explain them.

I saw Medouli several times more, that week. Once I went hunting with him, on a most beautiful mare he lent me: Medouli dressed all in white, like a Sultan, a pair of gold spurs more than a foot long projecting behind his white riding-boots, mounted on a beautiful dappled Arab that danced, nickering, all the time, almost sweeping the ground with its great arched tail. What a lovely beast it was! And what a rider! With him rode the little cavalcade of his most faithful officers: lean little ferrety men, or fat and imperious; but none of them with that air of simple, melancholy majesty; that face so gentle, so cruel, so sensitive; that body, which—in concord with the almost cat-like grace of the horse—showed a beauty of movement as pure as the greatest of dancers could express.

The next morning, to my surprise, I found the mare I had ridden still in our stables. My uncle grinned.

"I have sent word," he said, "that she awaits the return of my Koran!"

By midday came Medouli's answer—no Koran, but a slave, leading that lovely dapple stallion, with a message: '*Since the mare is to live the rest of her life far from her native pastures, I have sent this old friend of hers to keep her company.*"

His own favourite mount—and what that means to an Arab, we all know! The gesture was superb: he would do anything, it meant, except the blasphemy of surrendering The Holy Book. Uncle Robert was beaten—as he seldom was, in a contest of will. He sent back the stallion, of course; but he kept the mare, whose money worth was much the same as that of the manuscript.

All this while they were meeting every day: but neither mentioned the subject.

The beginning of the week found me an admirer: but by

the end of it I had a worship of Medouli that was almost religious: I was as blindly in love with him as only a schoolboy can be with his hero. If the Devil had offered me a price, then, for my soul, I know very well what I should have asked. It would have been that the Kaid should take me back with him, beyond the Atlas, to the great palace he had just built in the fertile valley of Medoula.

Nor would that have been a small price to ask, even of the Devil. The valleys beyond the Atlas were closed to the European, absolutely. The survivors of the Globe Venture fiasco had travelled through the Sous, it is true—but in chains. Cunningham-Grahame had tried to reach Taroudant in disguise—and been imprisoned for three months in the Atlas, by the Kaid of Gendoufa. For even if the fanatical native of those localities were himself likely to allow the filthy Christian to defile his pure Moslem air, the sleek merchants of Tafilet and Marrakesh were not. There was a good round sum in silver dollars set on the head of any Christian adventurer. The caravans across the desert from Timbuctoo, their silver and slaves, their almonds and copper and ostriches: the returning caravans with cotton and clocks and gunbarrels, Lyons silks and Venetian mirrors: the profits of these were best kept in pious Moslem hands.

They were no fools, these merchants. They knew what follows on the heels of your lone, harmless, brave, lovable explorer—once he has seen something, and seen that it is good.

My uncle had travelled in many forbidding parts of the country, in strange disguises—as a dumb dancing-boy, the first year he had spent in the country on leaving Eton: as a donkey-driver: a priest: a merchant. His own name, too, was one to conjure with; he could go among many tribes, without disguises, with whom even their brother Moslem would have been unsafe. But even *he* had never been to Medoula.

He would not ask; nor would he go without leave, in disguise. His fear of discovery in that case would not have been the fear of death, which had never disturbed him much; it would have been the fear of injury to his friendship.

Naturally I never told him of my secret ambition; but he knew well enough how I worshipped Medouli. We were watching him once, going through the streets on a pacing mule, with his band of councillors behind him. The beggars redoubled their cries as he approached: loathsome cripples would crawl on their elbows to kiss his mule's hoof-marks, and pompous little officials would bend down to kiss the hem of his robe, as he rode by. (Are the Moors alone in attributing a kind of holiness to temporal greatness?)

We were watching this, I say, when my uncle turned to me with a queer smile.

"One night, some years ago, I was dining in the Savoy," he said. "At the next table were a party of the most repulsive-looking, contemptible creatures I have ever seen. They were all in full evening dress; and the women with them were the very worst that our country has to offer its guests. One man, in particular, caught my eye; he had long, muscular arms, a narrow chest decorated with an enormous diamond stud: his nose was big and hooked, like a Jew's, but his lips and the dirty whites of his hooded eyes showed Negro blood: his black hair sprouted evenly all over, as if he ordinarily kept his head shaved. I thought that never, even in a West-End restaurant, had I seen a man so disgrace a suit of evening clothes." My uncle laughed harshly, and added, "Who do you think it was?"

I had not the least idea, and looked at him wonderingly, but my uncle turned the conversation.

iii

Great were the festivities in honour of the Kaid's

impending return to Medoula. The tribesmen rode in, troop after troop, shouting and waving their silver-mounted flint-locks round their heads, and their camps sprang up on the slopes of the bare hillside. Every day foraging parties rode out and drove home in the evening sheep and cattle—traditional extortion from the long-suffering peasant. Soon, even the vast courtyard of the great new palace was filled with flocks, and strident with the voices of strangers.

But still, in the private apartments of the Kaid, one little group of men worked on, apparently undisturbed by all the clamour. They were mosaic workers; at their head, Bou Ahmed—a young man, slightly fat, with an ivory skin and black moustaches, a face full of sensitive intelligence—the greatest mosaic worker of his generation. For five years he had toiled with his gang of workmen; he must have covered almost an acre of wall and floor with his delicate and harmonious geometrical patterns, that shimmered in the palace shade like the skin of a mackerel. Now he was finished. But his face was impassive; you could not have told if he felt either exaltation or fear.

In the women's quarters everything was bustle. Old favourites preened themselves in new dresses; tried the effect of a Nottingham-lace over-garment on some brocade dress as stiff and shapeless as cardboard; quarrelled over jewellery; scrambled for a packing-case of Paris hats; punched and pinched angrily at the big Negresses, who ran this way and that at everybody's beck and call.

Demure in the background, the new arrivals sat: scared, big-eyed country-girls, snatched from the well-side at some remote oasis, and now dressed for the first time by sardonic eunuchs in unbelievable finery: among them, a hard-cheeked French woman with metallic yellow hair. Or there—pacing up and down in the shadow of a colonnade, with the flowing movements of a young leopard—goes a Soussi dancing-girl, her cheeks glowing pink under her clear, golden complexion; her body, even as she walks, hinting at the mobile strength of the acrobat.

In the kitchens, with their great hooded charcoal furnaces, the bustle was no less. Sheep were being roasted whole; or wrapped in wet clay and baked in holes in the ground. Quails and chickens by the score, and partridges, would be hidden in tall cones of the white mealy couscous. Almonds were crushed by the hundredweight, and their milk cooled in snow brought many miles from the mountains, to serve as drink. Rare spices were pounded in mortars; and sweet cakes of honey and nuts twisted into fantastic shapes like lovers'-knots.

In the miserable sun-baked mud villages round, all was bustle too. Fat tax-gatherers groaned, knowing that now from themselves too would taxes be gathered: and each hunted out an older robe than his neighbour's, that each might appear the poorest of their Master's faithful, unselfish servants.

In the village of El Tleta the old sheikh gnawed at his beard, consumed with misgiving. All night he had been up, hiding his money in the underground granaries—all, that is to say, except the cauldron of silver dollars he meant to take as a 'free-will' offering to his Lord. But even this 'free-will' offering might not buy him his Master's pleasure. Something further, he felt, must be done. It was then that he remembered young Abdselam—a farmer who, in spite of the sheikh's attentions, had somehow managed to prosper; who had attained the portentous wealth of three cows, and, at the price of two of them, had married one of the prettiest girls in the village. Now the old sheikh congratulated himself on his forbearance: that he had never 'eaten up' Abdselam before.

*

Abdselam was sitting quietly in the shade of his palm-leaf hut, after a day's hard work in the millet-fields, when the sheikh's men came. They drove away his remaining cow, without comment, and burnt his hut; and his wife,

Heba, they carried off—to go, with that cauldron of silver dollars, as the peace-offering to the Kaid.

But there were many Abdselams who contributed unwillingly to these great and loyal festivities; and no one noticed the gaunt and ragged young man, now suddenly reduced to poverty, as, staff in hand, he bounded along the rocky path behind the sheikh and his cavalcade towards the palm-shaded gates of Medoula.

*

At last the Kaid with his escort was sighted by scouts, coming through the pass in the crimson mountains. Then the hubbub was redoubled. As he approached Medoula, troop after troop of tribesmen thundered towards him at full gallop, some dancing on their horses' backs, or leaping from horse to horse as they rode. Right up to the Kaid they would charge, then haul their horses into a dead halt on their haunches, fire their flint-locks in the air with one instantaneous roar, and wheel away. As the Kaid dismounted at the gate a hundred notables, forgetting their age and paunches, prostrated themselves in the dust. Medouli, tired though he was (if such a man could tire) after his long journey through the mountains, went immediately to his audience-chamber, and sat there for three hours—receiving gifts, and dispensing justice.

Then, with a little Yale key, he let himself into the private wing of the palace.

The caterwauling of the excited women from their quarters reached him: but he did not turn that way. Instead he walked alone down the long, glistening corridor to where Bou Ahmed sat on his heels, like an unseeing carved figure, amongst the beauty he had been so long creating.

Medouli looked at the work carefully, with the eye of a brother artist. He had been right. There was no other work through the length and breadth of Morocco as fine as this.

There was something kindly, regretful, in the strange face of Medouli as he greeted the artist: and when he dined that night, Bou Ahmed alone dined with him, while even the greatest of his lieutenants stood round in respectful silence.

No honour could have been higher.

After dinner, when both had washed their hands in rose-water from a golden ewer, Medouli rose and took Bou Ahmed by the hand, simply, like a child. Together they walked away down the corridor to where the last of Bou Ahmed's work—the veiling boards freshly removed—was still dark with damp. Neither spoke, though each knew well what business was still between them.

Bou Ahmed knew his skill was unequalled. He knew that Medouli was not the man to suffer that another should ever command his services.

*

At last Medouli walked alone down the empty passage to his bedroom. It was a small room, without windows, and in strange contrast to the rest of the palace. Here was no mosaic; instead, white-washed walls. The only furniture was a Spanish brass bedstead, smothered in many curtains; a washstand with a tin basin, beside which lay a safety razor of solid gold; and hanging by the bed, its hilt near the pillow, its muzzle towards the door, a well-oiled, loaded, shining service revolver.

iv

I have said that it was during my school holidays that I first went to Morocco, but ill-health caused those holidays to be prolonged for more than a year. This year I spent with my uncle, but mostly in the North—in Fez, Tangier and Rabat. I picked up Arabic quickly; but it was the Arabic of the grooms who taught me (much to the amusement of the Sultan, when he first heard me speak: for it was rather as if a debutante at Buckingham Palace had replied to some gracious remark of her Sovereign in the language of a fish-wife).

Nearly all this while I did not see Medouli again despite the fact that he returned across the mountains after only the briefest stay in Medoula. For one thing, he was hand in glove with the French. His adherence to their cause was one of the biggest factors in the rapidity of their advance. The benefit was mutual; and, as the greatest Moor on their side, their victory naturally made him the greatest Moor in the whole country.

One price that he easily exacted for his half was the absolute inviolability of the territory of Medoula. He would keep his tribesmen in alliance with the French, but only on condition that no Frenchman ever attempted to set foot in his realm.

Medouli, as I have said, had long policies: he might have held out for twenty years, had he chosen to fight them, like his brother chieftains. Probably even they knew they would be beaten in the end; but what is defeat to the average Moor, if it is distant even a few years of happy warfare? Most would never hesitate: but Medouli did. He knew that the New Order was coming, he knew that he himself was the last of the Old: there would never again in the Country be barbaric chieftains like himself.

His three favourite sons he sent to Paris—two to study Mining Engineering, and one to study Economics.

Looking back, now, I feel there was a certain magnificence in this. There is a wide enough gap between any parent and child, Heaven knows; but Medouli was voluntarily widening that gap by a thousand years.

Much of his wealth, too, was invested in the Banque de France; or in the blocks of office buildings that were springing up at Rabat and Casablanca. Was this for security? Medouli had shown little wish for security in the past.

As for the French, of course, they saw a different kind of security in all this. With Medouli's sons in the hands of their teachers, and his wealth in the hands of their bankers, they presently felt that they had him—so! That he could not escape them.

But, astute as they were, this was a blind way of looking at the character of Medouli.

He played up to them of course; it suited his purposes for them to *think* they had him on a line, since it was the only terms on which they would trust him. But he knew, he alone knew, that he was free as air. For there was a bedrock of asceticism in that great voluptuary which no one— except, perhaps, my uncle—suspected. It was the last trump card that he held. A great lover of magnificence, a lover of wealth, of power, of beauty, yet, had the French ever pushed him to the last resort, ever demanded of him something he was determined not to give, he was prepared, in his spirit he was fully prepared, to walk out on them; to leave everything in their hands that they thought he most valued: and, an ageing man, start life again as my uncle had first found him, with no other property than a gun, a ragged jelaba, and his belief in God.

It was hardly to be expected that his fanatical followers would see eye to eye with him in all he did. One and all would have preferred it if he had called upon them to follow him in a desperate Holy War; to burst through the mountains, loot Marrakesh and the rich Jews of Mogador, and drive the hated Christians into the sea. The biggest danger of rebellion, of course, he averted by forbidding any Christian to enter their country: but naturally the more intelligent amongst them were not ignorant of the general trend of his diplomacy; and, while he was away in the North, the hands of his *khalifas* were pretty busy keeping the murmurings within bounds. The ring-leaders found it easy to stir up discontent among the victims of robbery and extortion—robbery and extortion for which they themselves were often more directly responsible than their overlord, and by which, at least, they had certainly profited. It was only the exhibition of one of these ringleaders (to which the populace were presently treated), carried round from village to village in an iron cage, his hands split with leather thongs, that prevented discontent from becoming open revolt.

It was strange that amongst these growling conspirators young Abdselam, who had suffered so much, was not to be found.

After that one agonised evening which had seen him, bounding like a wolf, in the dusk, behind the cavalcade that carried his beloved Heba to the Kaid's palace, he seemed to have accepted his lot with true Mohammedan fortitude. Having no longer land of his own to till, he hired himself out as a labourer to the very sheikh who had dispossessed him—binding himself to twelve months' service for a miserable wage. Only if you had seen him some evening on the hillside, squatting immobile on his heels in the shade of a wild olive, his eyes fixed on the far away red walls of the Kaid's palace, would you have guessed that for him the past was not wholly past and done with.

But, after all, what could he do? A powerless, dispossessed man, even if he successfully immolated himself on the altar of revenge in some wild attempt at murder, what hope had he of ever seeing Heba again? What hope had he more than the other hundreds of victims of oppression, whose little wealth had gone to help rear that huge pile? Little hope, you might say. But Abdselam had cunning, and moreover he was in no hurry.

Meanwhile, within the palace walls, pacing courtyards where laden orange-trees shadowed splashing fountains, or sprawling on mountainous piles of cushions with the other girls (all of them apparently as ignorant of ennui as twiddling gold-fish in a bowl), the lovely Heba, too, ate out her life in hope. What use to her was her beauty? What good was it that she had been carried off from her penurious boor of a husband and set in a palace, if she had not so much as seen her new Lord? Had never had the chance to exercise her charms upon him, and secure for herself favours above those won by the ugly little minxes with thick ankles who now tyrannised over her?

*

It was not till the eve of my return to England that I saw Medouli again. It was the first time that he and my uncle had met for many months: for the French were jealous friends, and unwilling to believe that he could wish to see an influential Englishman in private for any other reason than to plot against them. Medouli, however, was now on his way back to the South, from which news had reached him that the unrest was reaching dangerous proportions, for the second time in a year. My uncle was an old man, and his health was bad; and I think that Medouli foreboded that they might never meet again. Moreover, I think even he felt it a relief to be a while with someone whom he did not need to deceive—either by speech or silence.

The three of us dined quietly in the house which my uncle had rented in Rabat, looking across the mouth of the river to Salé—that great stronghold of the Barbary Pirates, where Robinson Crusoe had once served as a slave.

But, somehow, everything did not go smoothly between the two friends that evening; and once my uncle burst out in downright anger. They had been discussing mosaic, and my uncle had asked him what became of the great Bou Ahmed, whom he had last heard of as working at Medoula. My uncle, it seemed, was anxious to employ him.

In his reply Medouli purred gently like a cat: "It is true," he said, "that I promised you Bou Ahmed, when he finished his work with me, should serve you before any of the other patrons who are clamouring for him. Can you not imagine, then, how embarrassing it was for me that he should die, as he did, the night his work was done, and that I should have to disappoint you all?"

My uncle went rather white and his old eyes flashed; but all he said, in a quiet voice, was: "And where did he die?"

"He died," said Medouli, "in front of the last piece of work he had done."

Old age and illness was telling on my uncle: he lost his temper, a thing he would never have done when he was a younger man, and rated his friend in language which would only have been suitable—indeed, only intelligible—to another European:

"That is the vulgarest thing you have ever done, Sidi. An act worthy of some petty, jealous little *nouveau riche*: an act of the grossest snobbery!"

I have said that such language would be unintelligible to a Moor, and so it was: for experience of such great vicissitudes of fortune as they suffer—where the rich governor of one day may be a common prisoner in the jail the next; or the beggar's son rise to lead a victorious army, and then leave his decapitated head to fester on the gate of some despised Jew—has left no room for snobbery as we know it. For snobbery like ours is a child born only of security in the tenure of property.

But Medouli answered reasonably enough:

"I do not think," he said, "that it was only jealousy made me act as I did. You see, Bou Ahmed well knew, five years ago, when he began the work, that he would not live after it was completed. (If he had not undertaken it, he would have died there and then.) Knowing that it was the last work he would do, is it reasonable to suppose that he would work with more application than otherwise he might ever have done in his life? For if an artist feels that *this* piece of work may be bad, but, with the help of Allah, next time he will do better, then he will always leave imperfections in his work. But if he feels, as Bou Ahmed, 'This piece of work is bad; with the help of Allah I must correct it, for I shall never have another chance,' then will he indeed produce (as Bou Ahmed has produced) his own everlasting memorial! I am a real patron of Art, Sidi."

Something of his meaning my crude Arabic was sufficient to follow; and I sat back aghast at his strange reasoning, realising for the first time the gulf which no romantic feeling would ever be adequate to cross. That my uncle regretted his outburst was plain, and the rest of the meal passed on indifferent topics, until it was nearly time for Medouli to leave. Indeed, the car that was to take him as far as the state of the roads allowed was already at the door. My uncle, referring to Omar's return to his own country, and hardly thinking, I suppose, what he said, murmured some conventional phrase to the purpose that Medouli would be glad to get back. Then it was the Kaid's turn to break out: I had never seen him moved before.

"To get back!" he said, with violent heat: "to get back —to what?" Medouli's dark face was working with excitement. "To get back to my own country, to people as savage as myself? As you know, I have no need for more wealth. The French think I give them my money to keep because I love it; because I want to make it safe. I give it to them because I do not care what becomes of it. Yet always I must have more. If I did not rob my people and extort from them, they would cry out that all change was against the will of Allah—To get back, then, to what? To my palace? What use are soft pillows to me? No pillow fits my head so comfortably as my saddle: there is no music like that of powder-play. To my women then? There are a thousand women in my harem at Medoula: all my life I have been collecting women, but what use are they to me now? I do not even care to look at them. The last time I went to Medoula, fifty homes were violated that I should have new women. There they live in my palace, and probably I shall never bother to see them. But that, too, I could not prevent: it is the custom!"

Medouli by now had forgotten my presence, and, leaning forward, fixed his burning eyes on his old friend, his arms on the table in front of him—forgetting, for once, even to hide his shrivelled left hand.

"I will tell you something, Penn," he said, "that you do not know. All my life I have been looking for one thing: a thing so simple that you Christians cannot imagine what it is like to be without it—a woman that I could talk to. I know now that I shall never find one. Do you know what happens if I speak to one of my women? She says to herself: 'I have found favour in the eyes of my Lord, I will ask for a new necklace!' There is not, among those thousand women, one woman who can think of anything else!"

He paused, and than added in a sombre tone: "My sons have all been begotten in silence."

It was a strange thing to sit there and watch the face of this father of two hundred sons, as he confessed his hidden, unfulfilled ambition: in the strangest way it had taken on the beautiful, young and wistful look of a child who first thinks of love; and sitting there beside that savage old voluptuary I felt myself—a fifteen-year-old schoolboy—to be old and cynical in comparison.

We were all silent. Then Medouli rose, kissed my uncle and, without another word, was gone.

v

Abdselam was in no hurry. His days were spent working for his master: at night (for he slept little) he would sit alone under the ancient wild olive on the hill above the village, thinking of his wrongs and his revenge. He had little imagination; but what little he had, jealousy intensified with a fiery heat. He was always thinking of Heba, his wife; who loved him alone, and could never love anyone else. She was the most beautiful woman in the world—he had no doubt of that. And then he would rack his brains to think how it could have come about that—careful as he was—the Kaid had somehow caught sight of her. Had he ridden by one day when she was working in the fields, or fetching water from the well? But surely if a man had passed she would have veiled herself, so that there would be nothing to distinguish her from the other, the plain country wenches. Yet somehow the Kaid *must* have seen her; or he would never have sent orders (for Abdselam supposed him to have sent) that she was to be carried off. Would never have installed her (as simple Abdselam supposed her to be installed) as the pride and queen of all the women in his palace.

One night, as Abdselam sat there, a strange sound rose to him from the ravine beneath—An enormous purring, rising and falling rhythmically, like music. Peering from the shadow of his tree he saw, in the soft moonlight, a lioness stretched out by the side of the pool, slowly kneading the sand, as a cat kneads a hearthrug, purring without pause. Abdselam's gun was at his shoulder; and then he saw something else. Silhouetted against the sky on a rock, a great black-maned lion was stalking up and down, backwards and forwards like a lion in a cage, looking into the distance. The purring grew louder and more insistent: the lion suddenly stopped; and stood, for a moment, as still himself as a rock. Then, roaring like a trumpet, he sprang —a clear leap forty feet through the air, landing with his teeth buried in the scruff of the lioness's neck.

But from the thicket beneath Abdselam came another sound, like the whetting of a knife on a grindstone; that ominous sound a wild boar makes, grinding his tushes before he charges. The Moors say that he is warning his enemy when he does that; they will tell you that they have even heard him say the words: 'Get ready, my enemy, for I am the Father of Tushes, and I disdain to kill you unprepared!'

Neither beast heard the warning, however; and the boar, hurtling on them like a thunder-bolt, caught them unexpectedly. The fight was one of the most terrific things

a hunter can ever see. The boar knows no fear; he alone
will challenge a lion, like this, to combat. Smaller than a
small donkey he must, nevertheless, have weighed a full
quarter of a ton: and in his first charge a boar goes faster
than any horse. The frightful impact drove his tushes deep
into the lion's side, while his own flanks, as hard as oaken
boards, seemed impervious to the slashing of the lion's
mighty claws.

Abdselam's old muzzle-loading flint-lock was hardly
adequate to deal with three such mighty beasts, and he
crept quietly home, meditating on what he had seen.

The Father of Tushes, for all his valour, is after all a pig
—the most unclean of animals to a Mohammedan: yet it
was from this foulness that the King of Beasts was to meet
his end.

*

The following evening, when his work was done,
Abdselam presented himself before the old sheikh, who
sat in the door of the square mud hut from which he
dominated the palm-leaf dwellings of the other villages.

After saluting him, he said: "I must leave your service,
Sidi."

"You bound yourself for a year," said the sheikh; "and
only eight months have passed. In four months more you
can leave my service if you like, but not now."

"Nevertheless," said Abdselam stubbornly, "I must
leave your service, Sidi."

"Have you a reason?" said the sheikh.

"I have a good reason," answered Abdselam, "and if
you knew it you would not only give me permission to
leave you, you would order me to do so."

"And this reason?" said the sheikh.

"That I cannot tell you, Sidi," replied Abdselam.

"I do not like people to have reasons they will not tell
me," rejoined the sheikh, menacingly. "If you will not

say, then you shall indeed leave my service—by way of the cemetery."

Abdselam appeared to consider the matter. "Then let me speak to you alone," he said.

The sheikh sent his attendants to a little distance, and Abdselam, even now not approaching too close, spoke confidentially.

"Do you remember, Sidi," he asked, "my wife, Heba, who, by your kind offices, found favour in the sight of our Lord the Kaid?"

Then he broke off, as if a new fear possessed him:

"Will you promise, Sidi, not to repeat to anyone what I am about to tell you?"

"I promise," said the old sheikh glibly, stroking his beard.

"She was a leper," said Abdselam.

The old man started as if he had been stabbed.

"I thought," said Abdselam, "that I had discovered the disease that very day; but I was not sure. Now, however, I am sure; for I am a leper too."

The old man sat in a heap, like a sack of flour, his mouth open and his eyes popping, while Abdselam drew back and then asked him again in a steady voice:

"Now may I leave your service, Sidi?"

With that the sheikh seemed to come to life.

"Yes, begone! Leave the village! Do not touch me! Begone!" he babbled, and called to his men to drive Abdselam out from the village with stones.

But Abdselam was already gone: in a couple of bounds he had disappeared in the dusk, and midnight found him hidden, his gun across his knees, at his old post under the wild olive tree. How long would it be before the sheikh told? Months, perhaps: he would be too fearful at his own part in the affair to do so at present. But Abdselam was in no hurry, he could wait. Of one thing he was certain— that the old fool would break his promise of secrecy some- time, and then the argument was simple: if he had caught leprosy from Heba, and now she was favourite in the Kaid's harem . . . The terror of leprosy was so overpowering that no leper—peasant or Kaid—was likely to be suffered by the tribesmen long to remain in their midst.

vi

That summer was a terrible one in the valley of Medoula, a foretaste of what was to come. During the winter little rain had fallen; and on the distant peaks, where it usually glistened well into May, the snow was all melted on these Southern slopes before March was out. The torrents which usually roared down the ravines in spring were little more than trickles this year; and by midsummer many of the wells—which depended for their water on moisture collected on a floor of rock some twenty feet below the sand —had begun to fail. Only in the palace fountains was water still plentiful, for it was brought there in ditches right from the mountains themselves: but if the surrounding country dried up, clouds of sand would soon fill these ditches faster than any labour could clear them.

The crops were scant, and the stock of goods in the shops of the village pawnbrokers soon piled up high. By the autumn men and women alike were beginning to show the weakness and the irritable excitability of famine: while the children, their eyes too large, no longer shouted and scuffled on the village middens. Then came winter, and with it at last promise of rain: black clouds scudded overhead, whirled onwards by the hot south wind. And still they whirled on, across the mountains to the north: but not a drop of rain fell in Medoula. What children were still fit for it their parents sold North to the trainers of acrobatic troupes, for whatever few coppers they would fetch. Strange marabouts appeared, and heathen rain-makers practised their magical rites openly: for though Islam frowns on magic, the people of Medoula were a race of semi-white Aborigines, descendants of the Carthaginians, and still heathens under the skin.

It was then the old sheikh's nerve broke. The curse of Allah was on the people who let a leper rule over them. It was a strange and ridiculous sight to see the old man run through the village, crying like a child, and wailing his terrible secret at the top of his voice.

It was like a spark to tinder. In twelve hours the story had spread from the Sahara to the Atlantic. Abdselam had moved up into the mountains as the game receded before the drought; but even there the news reached him. Ragged and barefoot, his gun still crooked lovingly in his arm, he returned to the wild olive tree, whose leaves now drooped dryly like shabby strips of paper.

The Kaid himself, on his return, half-lapsed back into the fatalism in which he was born, and made little attempt to fight the drought which God had sent. He set guards over his aqueducts to prevent the peasants who came for water from trampling the banks flat (as, in their idiot way, they otherwise certainly would): and he gave orders that water from his fountains should be given free at the gates to man and beast. But water for the crops he could not give; and in spite of his orders his servants only allowed even a pint of water to those who could pay them handsomely for it.

More Omar never attempted. He might, perhaps, have applied to the French to send grain; but he knew what that would mean. Their price would be their immediate occupation of his territory: an occupation which he had come to look upon as sacrilege as great as the possession of the Holy Koran by my infidel uncle had seemed. Better half the population should die than that! For next year it would certainly rain. It *must* rain. And with rain prosperity would return. In a year or two, also, his sons would be back from Paris; and with their help a new source of wealth—the rich mineral deposits of the valley—would be opened up: but not opened up as usual by European speculators—opened up by Moslems who had learnt the skill of the Nazarene. If he could weather the next few years, Omar saw in his mind's eye his sons establishing a new and formidable State of Medoula, which could meet the European on his own terms. A State which might yet win back the whole Shereefian Empire from the French, and set the flame of his lamp of Islam burning brightly once more in the modern world. As for himself, he had no place in all that. Even while he planned for it he hated it—it was distasteful to the very marrow of his barbaric bones. When that time came he would abdicate and, even in his old age, start out again on his perennial quest—for a woman he could talk to.

A woman he could talk to . . . As he paced alone in the empty, shimmering corridors that were Bou Ahmed's memorial, Omar suddenly remembered the despised women in his own harem. Might not, even there, be the very woman for whom he was always looking? He turned and strode towards the women's quarters; so quietly, that the eunuch sentries sleeping at the door never even woke till he kicked one of them with his foot. Then he passed within.

*

The veiling of women in the East—that strange sense of modesty which will make an Arab woman lift the hem of her skirt to cover her lips at the approach of a stranger—seems always to excite the most pleasurable surmise in the Occidental breast: but few seem to have paused to consider what effect the veil must have on the face it covers. Fish that live for generations in caverns to which no light can penetrate lose their eyes: and faces which are never (or very seldom) exposed to public gaze, seem in the same way to lose all mobility: they become, indeed, as inexpressive as any other part of the body that is habitually covered. That is the greatest shock which comes to those who have had occasion to see respectable or prized Eastern women unveiled—greater, even, than the often elephantine girth of their ankles: the doll-like woodenness of those faces which have never learnt to smile or frown, to darken or lighten, in harmony with open conversation. It is not only that these faces have nothing to express, they could express nothing if they had.

As he appeared quietly amongst them this woodenness struck Medouli—used by now to Western drawing-rooms —anew. What hope had he of finding here what he sought; what he had never found, except among the males of his people? Yet here it seemed as if a menagerie of women from all parts of the world were gathered: Arabs in Paris dresses, a middle-aged German woman dressed as a Turk, great shining Negresses—there seemed a specimen of everything. And all clustered round him as he appeared, strutting and posturing; and demanding, if his eye so much as rested on them for a moment, the inevitable present—a new dress, a brooch or buckle, or the public discomfiture of a rival.

There were only two women there who were at all aloof. One—a young girl, half-Arab and half-Negress, beautiful as a hind—stood by herself, seeming to show neither fear of him nor eagerness to catch his attention. She was utterly absorbed, to the exclusion of every other possible thought or feeling, in her own admiration of her own dress. The other he did not see: the young Soussi acrobat, who had tumbled and swung on every stage in the world from Chicago to Port Said, hid indifferently behind a pillar.

For a few moments Medouli stood there hesitant, watching them, his eyes blank, his mouth open, with the vacant air of a dull-witted schoolboy who has not heard for half-an-hour one word the master has said.

There were so many of them that Heba, standing on tip-toe at the back, and clutching viciously at the shoulders of those in front of her, even then hardly caught a glimpse of him.

Then without a word Omar turned to the door by

which he had entered: but even as he turned, the door burst open, and the Captain of the Eunuchs—his face ashen with fright—stumbled in.

"Master, the gate!" he cried. "Come quickly: they are forcing the gate!"

*

Abdselam, the outcast and self-styled leper, had left the wild olive and taken up his post on a nearer hillock. He saw the crowd of fear-maddened tribesmen surging round the gate: thundering on the huge iron-plated doors. Then he saw them draw back, and with their guns shoot the lock to pieces. He guessed, from the roar of the one word 'leper!', when the Kaid's lonely figure must have crossed the court within to meet them. He heard the ensuing volley.

Then followed such a scene of pillage as can seldom have been witnessed. But in that he took no interest. He knew that whatever became of the other women, no one would dare to touch Heba: that she would be driven out—a bewildered outcast, not even knowing why. And, as he sat there, he presently saw her stumbling figure run from the palace in his direction.